EVERY NINE SECONDS

it's even better the second time!

queer as folk
THE COMPLETE SECOND SEASON

own it on dvd and home video!

over 3 hours of specially produced features:

- ▶ folks on the road: a backstage pass
- ▶ a day in the life of **queer as folk**
- ▶ the making of **rage gay crusader**
- ▶ wrap party reel
- ▶ video jukebox
- ▶ season 3 sneak peek

new episodes
sundays 10 pm et/pt

a **queer**as**folk**

novel

EVERY NINE SECONDS

Joseph Brockton

POCKET BOOKS
New York London Toronto Sydney Singapore

An *Original* Publication of POCKET BOOKS

 POCKET BOOKS, a division of Simon & Schuster, Inc.
1230 Avenue of the Americas, New York, NY 10020

ISBN: 0-7434-7612-3

First Pocket Books trade paperback printing March 2003

10 9 8 7 6 5 4 3 2

For information regarding special discounts for bulk purchases, please contact Simon & Schuster Special Sales at 1-800-456-6798 or business@simonandschuster.com

Printed in the U.S.A.

For Vinnie Levin and Brittany Lynn

*. . . they say men think about sex every
twenty-eight seconds.
Of course, that's straight men.
With gay men, it's every nine.*

—MICHAEL NOVOTNY (EPISODE 1)

chapter one

Michael Novotny sat on his bedroom floor wearing his Captain Astro pajamas and inhaling deeply on the last remnants of a joint. The fumes slid between his lips, down his throat, and into his lungs. He held the smoke there and handed the joint back to his best friend, Brian Kinney.

He tried not to laugh, since that would release the smoke and totally ruin the effect.

The superhero pajamas had been a gift from his mother. She had sewn them together out of material she had unexpectedly stumbled across a month before his last birthday. It had taken her a couple weeks to finish the simple outfit since she had to find time to work on it between shifts of her job at the Red Robin Diner and while Michael was at school.

The pajamas were supposed to have been a gag gift. She gave them to her son on his eighteenth birthday. The day he supposedly became a man.

He hadn't gotten the joke.

Brian lifted the joint to his mouth. The paper bonded with his lips as he closed his eyes and inhaled, savoring the familiar taste.

Brian wasn't dressed in superhero pajamas.

He wasn't dressed in much at all.

A pair of tight white Calvin Klein briefs barely concealed his ample bulge. The material of his white CK T-shirt strained against a chest that was trying to burst out of the fabric. His tanning-bed-darkened skin stood out in contrast to the pure white of his clothing.

It was the only thing pure about him.

Brian had learned the value of a good workout years earlier, and his body displayed that fact proudly. His hair was mussed, but still neatly trimmed. He wore it short and deceptively simple as if to make up for the years he had had it feathered on the sides. The entire look was well cultivated to walk the line between boy and man.

He snuffed out the last of the roach.

The two young men exhaled together. The smoke intermingled between them.

Michael liked the buzz. He felt much calmer than he normally did when Brian was in his bedroom. He also felt hornier. The room seemed more alive to him in the darkness that was lessened only by the light of a street-lamp streaming in through the window.

It was eight minutes to midnight on the night before Brian Kinney's eighteenth birthday. Brian had a standing invitation to stay over at Michael's house whenever he chose. And he chose to do so often. It didn't matter that it was a school night. Brian's parents had given up on keeping track of him years ago.

Besides, the school year was almost over. The Susquehanna High School class of 1989 were less than a month away from their freedom. And Brian was always slightly ahead of his peers.

"So when do I get my present?" Brian asked as the last wisp of smoke brushed past his lips.

Michael tried to put off the inevitable. "It's not your birthday yet."

"It's *always* my birthday."

Michael couldn't argue with that logic. Brian was always celebrating his life in one way or another—often in his birthday suit. Michael uncrossed his legs and got up off the floor. He had the two small, wrapped gifts under his pillow.

"Happy eighteenth birthday," Michael said with his usual exuberance. "It isn't much."

"It's from you, Mikey. It's more than enough."

Michael sat back down as he handed Brian the gifts. He wished that the presents didn't look so small, but took some solace in the fact that his mom was always saying, "It's the thought that counts." Then again, he hadn't really put a lot of thought into the gifts. He knew the things Brian liked. Buying him gifts was easy. Michael hadn't bothered to get a card, knowing how Brian would react to the forced Hallmark sentiment or stupid cartoon humor.

"What have we got here?" Brian coyly asked as he took the gifts out of Michael's hands. He opened the smaller one first. It was plainly in the shape of a cassette.

"It's a mix tape," Michael said as the wrapping came off.

"I can see that." Brian read the names written on the side. "The Cure, Prince, Echo and the Bunnymen . . . Rick Springfield?" He looked up at Michael. "That's quite a mix."

"They're from different points in our friendship," Michael said, grinning.

"Put in on." Brian handed the tape to Michael.

"Okay." Michael slid over to his Casio boom box and slipped the tape in. He adjusted the volume controls so it wouldn't disturb his mom, who was sleeping just down the hall. It didn't really matter, though. The walls of the house were so thin that she could probably hear everything that was going on in Michael's room anyway.

She could probably smell the pot too.

Brian held the remaining small square box and gave it a shake. Something inside rattled against the cardboard. "Pot pipe?" he asked with a smile.

"Yeah, my mom picked it up for me," Michael sarcastically replied.

The Smiths started playing on the boom box: "The Boy with the Thorn in His Side."

Brian tore the wrapping off the second box and dropped it on the floor. He lifted the lid and found a leather bracelet with a ring of small white shells. It wasn't a typical Brian Kinney fashion accessory, but when Michael had first seen it, something about the bracelet had just seemed perfect.

"I got it at that craft show mom dragged me to last week at the Expo Center in Greengate," Michael said. "I know it's not really your—"

"I love it." Brian slid the bracelet onto his wrist. "Thank you, Mikey." He gave his friend a quick peck on the cheek.

Brian was quite a picture—almost naked except for his barely fitting underwear and the bracelet on his wrist. Michael was enjoying the view.

Four minutes to midnight.

"Almost eighteen," Brian said with a level of excitement that he rarely allowed anyone to see.

"Like it makes a difference."

"It makes all the difference in the world, Mikey. High school's almost over. College is just around the corner. A whole new life."

Michael hated that Brian was so excited about the future. They were heading off to very different schools.

Brian had received a full soccer scholarship to Carnegie Mellon University. Michael would be attending Allegheny Community. While the two schools were relatively close to each other, this "whole new life" could mean the end of their friendship.

To make matters worse, Brian had been accepted for an early session.

He would be moving into his dorm in only a month.

"I was thinking," Michael said, cautiously approaching a subject he had been planning to suggest for a while. "About Captain Astro and Galaxy Lad."

"When aren't you?" Brian asked, but there was no condescension in his voice. He no longer shared Michael's interest in comic books, but he never begrudged his best friend the indulgence.

"In issue forty-four, *The Bond of Brotherhood,* Galaxy Lad suggested they take a blood-brother oath to cement their friendship. I was thinking we could do the same thing." Michael got off the floor and stepped over to his desk. He rifled through the top drawer. "We could use my dad's Swiss Army knife."

"Knives and bloodletting?" Brian chuckled. "I didn't know you were into S and M."

"Only on special occasions." Michael sat back down with the knife in his hand. It was one of the few things he had that had belonged to his father, who died in Vietnam. Using a fingernail, he opened the knife and moved the blade toward his thumb. "Now we just have to—"

"Hold it." Brian grabbed the knife from his friend. "If we're going to do this, we should do it right." He picked up the Bic that they had used to light the joint and flicked it on. An orange glow lit their faces as Brian moved the blade across the flame. His eyes locked with Michael's as fire burned the blade clean.

Brian removed his thumb from the lighter and the flame was extinguished. He dropped the Bic to the floor.

And waited.

Michael tried to focus on The Smiths as the clock ticked toward midnight. He wasn't sure about what Brian had in mind.

And when you want to live
How do you start?

"Give your thumb a little prick," Michael said.

Brian raised an eyebrow but let the pun slip away unspoken. "Michael, blood oaths like that are for straight little Boy Scouts." He slowly rose off the floor, indicating to Michael to rise as well.

They stood facing each other with only a few inches between them.

"Are you ready to take a real pledge, Mikey?" Brian moved the blade between them.

"What are you—"

Brian held the blade up to Michael's lips, shushing him. "Do you trust me?"

"Yes," he answered without even thinking.

"Silly rabbit." Brian guided the knife down past Michael's chin.

The blade came to the bottom of the V in the neck of Michael's pajama top. Brian gathered the fabric in his hand and pulled it away from Michael's body. With a flick, Brian sliced through the threading and the top button fell to the floor.

"Brian—"

"Shhh."

The blade dropped an inch to the next button, which came off with a pop. The third and fourth buttons followed in short order. Michael inhaled sharply as the cool air hit his chest. It was smooth. His pecs were just beginning to take on a more masculine shape.

Normally, Michael would be uncomfortable to be so exposed around Brian, but his mind was elsewhere at the moment. Blood was coursing through his body and away from his brain. It all seemed to be heading toward one particular place.

The last button came off. A line of flesh peeked out from between the flaps of his pajama top. His stomach was taut.

Brian brushed against Michael's erection as his free hand grabbed at the lone button on the pajama bottoms. Michael sucked in more air, wondering just how far this was going to go. He was both nervous and excited.

The blade pressed up against the button.

If the bottoms came off, he wondered, what would happen next? There was a lot of activity between his and Brian's crotches. He couldn't be sure, but he thought he saw the outline of Brian's erect penis in his white CK's. He looked back into Brian's eyes.

His face registered the silent plea: *Do it.*

Brian released the fabric without cutting the button.

A wave of disappointment mixed with relief flowed through Michael.

But Brian wasn't done.

The blade was in front of Michael's face once more. He was tempted to ask what the hell was going on, but he didn't want to spoil the mood. Brian was in control. Michael was just along for the ride. He wasn't concerned. Brian always made him feel safe.

Michael could feel the blade gently pressing against his temple. The metal was still warm from the fire it had been through. He could feel the edge of the blade as it slid down the side of his face. Brian was putting just enough pressure on the handle so that Michael would feel it, but it would not leave a mark. The blade traced along the jawline, ending beneath his chin.

Michael stole a glance at the clock. It was only seconds until Brian's birthday. Even though he hadn't seen Brian look at the time, Michael knew his friend was aware of the passing seconds.

A brief flicker of pain brought his eyes back to Brian.

Michael's lips felt wet. His tongue ventured out and was met with a coppery taste. Brian had cut Michael's bottom lip.

He looked to his friend about to question what was going on when he noticed a matching small cut on Brian's lip. Before Michael could say anything, Brian leaned forward and the two cuts met.

Brian had kissed Michael many times before on the cheek and forehead, and even a couple brushes on the lips. They were nothing like this kiss. Michael felt passion and intensity and Brian's tongue pushing to get into his mouth.

Michael's experience with boys was limited to say the least. He had never even had a real kiss before. Michael opened his mouth to let in the welcome guest. Blood and saliva intermingled.

It was unlike anything Michael had ever imagined. He thought it impossible for his dick to get any harder, but it did with each passing second. He wanted to push his body up against Brian's, but fear kept him at a safe distance.

Typically, a scene like this would end one of two ways.

Option A: The flimsy material between the two boys would be torn away and their naked bodies would glow in the moonlight. Brian would then guide Michael over to the bed and lead him through a night of either passionate lovemaking or intense sex.

Option B: Michael would wake up.

But this was no dream.

This was Brian Kinney.

This was Michael Novotny.

And this was their friendship.

Brian opened his eyes and pulled away. A thin line of blood briefly linked their silent pledge. When it broke, the invisible bond remained.

Michael pressed his lips together to savor the kiss before he accepted that the moment had ended.

"Time for bed, Mikey," Brian said.

It wasn't an invitation for more.

Brian got into bed.

Michael's disappointment abated slightly when he saw the tiniest little wet spot right below the elastic of Brian's briefs as the thin sheets covered his body. Brian had been turned on by what had just happened.

Michael's own underwear was rather moist as well.

He slid under the sheets beside Brian on the twin bed. Their bodies shared the space in the middle as they had many times before. Only a few inches separated them. Michael could feel the cut on his lip already closing over.

Brian was lying on his side with his back to Michael. The sheets rose and fell as he breathed. Michael mirrored Brian's position, hoping that his friend would lean back into him. He wanted to touch Brian, but was too afraid to make the move. Sometime in the middle of the night they would fall into each other as they normally did, but Michael never had the courage to make that happen intentionally. He would have to settle for waking with Brian's arm around him or his head on Brian's chest.

It was as if their sleeping bodies had better sense than their waking minds.

The music had shifted to the second song on the mix tape.

Patrick Swayze sang them off to sleep.

chapter two

Michael's erection woke him before the alarm clock went off. He enjoyed the friction of his body against the bed for a few thrusts before he realized that he was alone. As his eyes blinked open, he tried to get accustomed to the light coming in the window, which was still open. The cool Pittsburgh morning air kept him under his sheet. The scent of pot from the night before still lingered.

He didn't want to move. It was too comfortable in bed, and as long as he stayed there, he could replay the events from the previous night over and over in his mind without interruption. When he had first thought of bringing up *The Bond of Brotherhood*, he had figured that Brian would just laugh at him, which made no sense at all. Brian rarely ever laughed at Michael. But

that was just the way Michael's mind worked sometimes. Things had gone far better than he had thought
they would. He and Brian now had a piece of each other
that they would carry for the rest of their lives. That
thought rolled through his mind as he stretched out on
his Captain Astro sheets wishing for a few more minutes of rest.

Unfortunately, he did have to get to school. Although
the school year had unofficially ended already, the students
were still required to show up for a few more weeks until
the actual graduation ceremony. It was one of the lamer
school rules Michael knew that he was legally required to
follow and the reason he had to get up. Then again, he also
wanted to find out what had gotten Brian out of bed so
uncharacteristically early.

Michael pushed aside the sheet and dropped his bare
feet onto the floor. The old rug scratched against his toes
as he stood. He crossed over to the window and closed it,
shutting out the chilly spring morning.

"Michael, are you up?" his mom yelled from downstairs. She had probably heard his footsteps.

"Yeah!" he yelled back.

"I'm making breakfast! Hurry up."

The smell of bacon already filled the house.

Michael was one of the lucky few students at
Susquehanna High with a mom who made breakfast
every morning. At least, every morning that she didn't
have to work the early shift at the diner. The trade-off

was that he was expected to do some of the more "manly" chores around the house like cleaning the gutters and mowing the lawn. That was fine with him. It was a role he had taken on early in life and the trade-off was worth it. He didn't even think Brian's mom knew how to cook. It was okay, though. It just meant his friend would come over more often for a home-cooked meal.

He scratched at his chest and nether region and realized that he couldn't go downstairs dressed as he was. It was going to be hard to explain to his mom how he had managed to lose all the buttons on his pajama top so soon after she had sewn it for him. She took pride in her work and would insist on knowing the cause of their removal. He collected the buttons off the floor and then removed the pajamas, putting everything into a pile in the corner to worry about later. He threw on a pair of sweatpants and a baggy T-shirt.

The sweats rode up his ankles a bit due to his minor growth spurt from the previous summer. Michael still wasn't as big as Brian, but he did finally stand taller than his mom. He brushed his hand through his hair to rid himself of bed head. The previously curly black hair had managed to straighten itself out a bit through puberty, but still rebelled from time to time.

Michael hurried downstairs to find a plate of scrambled eggs, toast, and bacon waiting for him in the kitchen along with his mom. She was standing over the table wearing her black-and-white waitress uniform, setting another plate across from his seat. Brian, however, was nowhere to be found.

"Is that for Brian?" Michael asked, although he suspected not because his mom's copy of Danielle Steel's *Star* was sitting beside the plate.

"Actually, I thought I'd cook something for myself. Crazy, huh?"

"Did he eat already?"

"He was out the door before I could even turn on the stove. Must be in a rush to celebrate his birthday."

"I guess." Michael dug into breakfast.

"Don't know what kind of celebrating he could do so early in the morning." She sat across the table from her son. She was obviously pressing for information in her usual not-so-subtle way.

"Beats me."

"So what do you boys have planned for tonight?" she asked between bites of her eggs.

"Beats me." He chewed on a piece of bacon.

"Sounds like fun. You guys have fun last night? And if you say 'beats me,' you're going to be wearing those eggs."

Michael could sense that the conversation was leading somewhere. "We just hung out."

"You know I don't like you burning incense in your room, right?"

"Sorry," he said, knowing that she was well aware that it wasn't incense.

"Remember"—she wagged her finger at him—"just say no . . . to incense."

Even when scolding him, Michael's mom always found a way to make him laugh. Of course, after the laughter, silence hung over the table for a moment while Debbie purposely let the comment hang in the air. Michael focused on his scrambled eggs, unable to look his mom in the eye. He didn't like getting her looks of disappointment. Fortunately, it didn't happen often.

"So, is anyone else going tonight?" she asked, giving her son a reprieve. "Or is it just you and Brian again."

"Probably just us. Why?"

"No reason," she said, although there seemed to be something more. "By the way, I managed to pull off a bit of a miracle. I'm working the day shift for the next month so I don't have to miss the prom or your graduation."

"How did you manage that?" Michael asked, truly shocked. The diner where his mom worked was open twenty-four hours, and the owner liked to rotate the waitresses' shifts weekly for reasons defying explanation. The day shift was always Debbie's favorite since she didn't have to go in until the middle of the breakfast rush, then stayed through lunch and left after helping set up for dinner. It was the closest thing to a nine-to-five job she would ever have.

"No thanks to that asshole Mulcahey," she said, referring to her boss. "I had to beg, borrow, and steal from the other waitresses to get them to switch shifts. Thank God

Rosie helped out. Speaking of which, you can give her ticket to the graduation to someone else since she's working that night for me. And be sure to thank her when you see her."

"Will do." Rosie Catalano was Debbie's closest friend at the Red Robin and, by default, was a friend of Michael's as well. She was one of the few adults he felt comfortable addressing by her first name. He would certainly remember to thank her. His mom would have been a mess if she missed his graduation.

"Oh, and I have some other news," she said.

"You're a regular Barbara Walters this morning."

"Don't be smart. When you were telling me about your senior class picnic, I got to thinking. That PFLAG group I go to is turning into a bunch of whiny old women . . . even the men. It's all tragedy this and moaning about that. So I was thinking of organizing a picnic so we could actually have some fun for a change."

Michael could see the direction this was going. Talk of one of her friends' "nice young son" was definitely in the making. "And how did this idea go over at the meeting?" he asked, hoping that it was about as popular an idea with the group as it was with him.

"Not well at all. Those old broads thought the idea of a picnic was too frivolous."

Michael buried his excitement.

"So," she continued, "I had a bit of a brainstorm. I convinced the *ladies* that we should have the picnic in honor of the twentieth anniversary of the Stonewall Riots in New York. You know, since that was kind of the start of the gay rights movement."

Actually, Michael didn't know, and he wasn't that interested in finding out.

"Good thinking," he said, more out of an obligation to speak than anything else.

"Speaking of the anniversary, did you know that the post office is issuing the first lesbian and gay pride postage stamp next month?" Debbie asked rhetorically, as she set off on another of her discussions on gay politics and history.

Michael didn't bother to tell his mom that he didn't really care. She just refused to accept that he was eighteen and wasn't really interested in the sociopolitical status of the homosexual cause. He had far more important things to worry about . . . like the prom. But, he respected his mom too much not to listen. Eventually, she seemed to exhaust the subject and moved on to discussing her plans for the garden.

The rest of their breakfast was filled with general conversation about nothing important. Once they finished, Michael helped his mom with the dishes before running back upstairs to get ready for school. Since Brian had left with his car, it meant that Michael would have to leave a little earlier to walk.

Susquehanna High School wasn't that far from Michael's house, but the walk seemed a lot worse ever since Brian had started giving him rides. Michael set out from his house with his backpack slung over his shoulder. The bag was fairly empty since teachers had stopped giving out homework a week earlier. At this point in the year, everyone was just coasting through to graduation.

Michael walked along the streets of Pittsburgh at a leisurely pace. He wondered what Brian had in mind for the birthday celebration. Brian had been keeping silent on the festivities, but Michael knew that the plans were going to be good. His best friend rarely showed excitement over anything, but whenever the subject of his birthday came up, Brian's enthusiasm was unlike anything else Michael had ever seen. Sometimes, it was infectious. Other times, it scared the fuck out of him.

When Michael reached the First Presbyterian Church, he took a seat on the steps out of habit. It was something he had done for the three and half years before Brian got his car. Once again, he wondered what Brian was up to.

"Well, isn't this a surprise," Lisa Ward said, standing over him.

"I thought we could have one last walk to school together," Michael said as he stood. "For old times' sake."

"Brian bailed on you, huh?" she said as they started walking together.

Michael had known Lisa since the first day of kindergarten. The moment his mom had tried to leave him at school, he started screaming and crying. Nothing his mom or the teacher could do would calm him down. Then Lisa came over and smacked him in the arm. *Shut up, already,* she had said. *Okay,* he'd replied, and calmed down. They were friends from that moment on.

The two of them used to "go out" in third grade. Not that they really went anywhere, but they did consider themselves a couple largely because they were inseparable. It was a few years before they both developed an actual interest in boys. Of course, Michael hadn't shared his little secret yet, but knew that Lisa would be the first person he told.

He had never told Brian or his mom. Somehow, they had already known.

Lisa's shoulder-length black hair waved behind her as she walked. Puberty had been good to her, just as it had been good to Michael. She was just a bit shorter than Michael and her body had taken on a pleasant shape. Her face was attractive but not quite beautiful and didn't require a lot of makeup to be appreciated.

"How's the article coming?" she asked, referring to the piece he was writing, "Growing Up in the Eighties," for their final issue of the school paper, the *Susquehanna Spotlight.* Lisa was the editor and Michael was her primary columnist.

"It's . . . um . . . it's getting there." It wasn't exactly a lie.

"Haven't started yet, huh?"

"I've been gathering research." That part was true. Michael had been going through his mom's old issues of *People* magazine that she kept in the garage. She liked to make fun of his comic book collection, and yet, her magazine collection was almost twice the size. She wouldn't even let him touch the special issues, such as the memorial tribute to Lucille Ball that had come out a few weeks ago. "There's a lot to go over."

"So I guess you won't be able to turn it in early. Like tomorrow?"

The request caught him off guard. He was never going to be able to write the article *and* celebrate Brian's birthday. "Tomorrow's Saturday."

"I know. But I really want the final issue of the *Spotlight* to be special. Since the class picnic is Monday, I was hoping I could get everything in a little early, so I can lay it out over the weekend."

Lisa tended to get a bit worked up about the paper. Considering that this was the very last issue that she would be editor of, he had expected her to be freaking out over it by now. But she had been considerably more mellow about life in general since she had gotten accepted into Penn State's journalism program.

"I'm not going to be able to get it done tonight," he said as they neared the school. Brian's birthday easily took precedence over any school-related work, even if it was for Lisa.

"Sunday's fine," she said without blinking.

"You really do have a problem taking no for an answer," he said as they reached the school grounds. "That's something you need to work on."

"Why? It's how I get what I want."

Michael smiled. He knew she was right. He also knew that he'd be handing in his article Sunday morning.

"Is noon okay?" he asked.

"Good enough."

Susquehanna High School stood before them in all its red-brick glory. The massive complex comprised a main building, several annexes, and sweeping grounds. The building itself was only two stories tall, but stretched out to cover a couple city blocks. Its sports fields, however, covered more land than the school itself, and that wasn't even including the football stadium.

"There's Christine," Lisa said when she saw another friend and member of the newspaper staff. "I've got to talk to her about the piece on where everyone is going to college."

"I think she saw you." Michael smiled. "Look, she's running away."

He wasn't entirely incorrect.

Lisa laughed at herself. "Okay, I know I'm a bit overbearing. I'll calm down."

Michael didn't say anything. He just waited.

"Oh, hell," Lisa said as she started running off. "Christine!"

Michael let out a laugh as he watched Lisa practically

tackle Christine. He would do his best to get his article to Lisa by Sunday so long as Brian's plans didn't interfere. As Michael walked into the school, he once again wondered where his friend was. It was unlike Brian to just disappear on Michael with no explanation. Sure, Brian pulled those disappearing acts often, but with other people, never with Michael.

He tried not to let it concern him as he worked the combination to his locker.

Michael smelled the trouble coming before he saw it. The scent of Drakkar Noir was a heavy cloud that moved through the halls of Susquehanna High. Michael wondered if he would spend the rest of his life dreading that smell.

Todd Weaver and his two cronies, Jason Burns and Steven Winter, were coming down the hall.

Michael braced for verbal impact.

"Hey, faggot," Todd yelled as he sauntered up. The stench of cologne grew even more pungent. "You excited that you get to wear a gown at graduation?"

Michael pulled on the latch and opened his locker with a slam. It would probably be more bearable if the insults were even remotely creative. He stuffed his book bag inside the locker and could almost hear Todd reloading for another lame insult. The rest of the hall was silent except for the laughter coming from Jason and Steven.

"Dude, maybe you can get under my gown and suck

me off during the ceremony," Todd bellowed through the hall.

"How would he ever find such a tiny prick in the dark?" Brian asked loudly as he came down the hall. This time, there was a bit more laughter. However, it wasn't coming from Jason or Steven.

Michael released the breath he hadn't realized that he had been holding.

"S'up, Brian," Todd simply replied as he swiftly made his way down the corridor with his friends in tow.

"*S'up*, yourself," Brian replied as he reached Michael's locker.

"Thanks," Michael said.

"Four years and you still take it. Are you ever going to stand up to him?"

"How does he know? It's not like I've ever told anyone." Michael shifted his books around in the locker. He was stalling. He didn't really need to get anything.

"He doesn't know. He just suspects enough to have some fun at your expense." Brian nudged his friend aside to check himself out in the mirror Michael had stuck on his locker door. Michael was pleased to see that Brian was still wearing the shell bracelet. "I mean, you're not exactly Joe Butch. And you do hang out with me, while my exploits with the soccer team are legendary, on and off the field."

"Not to mention your exploits with the soccer coach."

Brian turned on his friend. "Shut the fuck up," he said

in a strained voice just above a whisper. Then he reined in his temper. "You're the only one who knows about my . . . volunteering to help clean up the locker room from time to time. If anyone found out, Gary would be in a shitload of trouble." Brian returned to his primping. "The small-minded people of Pittsburgh wouldn't understand the nature of our friendship."

"Okay. Sorry."

"Apology accepted." Brian moved in to give his friend a peck on the cheek.

Michael dodged the move, checking up and down the hall to make sure none of their classmates had noticed.

"How do you get away with it?" Michael asked as he went back into his locker. "You're much more . . . active than me and no one picks on you."

"Well, the last guy that did wound up with a broken hand."

"That's what I mean." Michael closed the locker door and gave the lock a spin. "You broke the quarterback's hand last year in the middle of football season and totally got away with it."

"It helps that the team's record for the season was better once he was benched and Tony Nicolletti was brought in."

"I guess Tony kind of owed you for giving him a chance to play."

"Oh, he found a way to thank me." Brian started down the hall.

Michael chose to let the innuendo hang in the air without comment as he fell into step with Brian. "Where did you go this morning?"

"Just picking up another birthday present." Brian fished around in his pocket. He pulled out a set of cards and handed them to Michael. "One for me and one for you."

It was a pair of Pennsylvania driver's licenses.

"Where did you get these?" The one with Michael's picture on it looked exactly like the one he already had in his wallet, except that the date of birth was listed as 1968 as opposed to 1971. They were the most convincing fakes Michael had ever seen. They were the *only* fakes Michael had ever seen.

"I have connections," Brian replied.

Michael asked the next logical question: "*Why* did you get these?" They were both eighteen now, which meant that they were able to vote and enjoy more private adult activities without fear of repercussions. It also meant that they still weren't quite old enough to drink legally, but that had never before stopped Brian.

"There's a club opening tonight that I thought would be the perfect place to celebrate my birthday." They entered the stairwell that took them up to the second floor. "The only problem is we need to be twenty-one to get in." Brian took his ID back from Michael. "Problem solved."

Michael still couldn't get over the look of the IDs. Even

the hologram symbol of the Keystone State looked authentic. "How much did these cost?" Michael asked, trying to hide his concern that he couldn't really afford the luxury.

"It's been taken care of," Brian said instinctively, answering the unasked question.

"I thought your breath smelled suspiciously minty fresh," Michael said, throwing out his own innuendo.

"Someone's turning into a little smart ass." They stepped out of the stairwell. "I bought them with granny's birthday money."

"I'm sure she'd be happy to know that her gift was put to good use."

They continued down the hall until they reached the intersection where they had to split up to get to their respective classrooms.

"What do you want to do after homeroom?" Brian asked.

"Well, I was planning on going to first period. Unless you had something better in mind." Michael didn't usually like to cut school, but grades had gone in on Monday, so all they really had to do was show up for homeroom and sign in. Then they were free to go wherever they wanted. "We could go see *Road House* again. Another chance to check out Patrick Swayze's naked butt on the big screen."

"For the third time." Brian didn't sound too enthused. "I've got a better idea."

"Why do I always shudder when you say that?" Michael knew full well that he would do whatever Brian suggested. And that he'd probably have fun doing it.

"Meet me at the Nova after homeroom." Brian released Michael from his hold. "We need to look good tonight. We're going shopping."

chapter three

Brian leaned up against his 1962 Chevy Nova in the student parking lot. The pristine classic car with black body and white top stood out among the other students' beat-up cars from more recent years. He watched as several of those generic vehicles peeled out of the lot one after another, shaking his head at his fellow classmates' lack of style.

Cars weren't exactly Brian's "thing." He couldn't cite the make or model of a vehicle just by looking at it. He didn't spend weekends working under the hood checking the oil. But he did know what looked good. The Nova was a piece of art, but more than that, it was his freedom. The car got him where he wanted to go. Mainly, that was just getting him the hell out of the house.

Brian's mind flickered briefly to his home, if it could

even be called that. He hadn't been there in several days. He much preferred staying with Michael and his mom. The atmosphere was considerably more homelike, and the food was pretty good too, although Debbie tended to force more of it on him than he wanted. Brian wondered if his parents were planning anything for his birthday. He didn't think they were and actually hoped that they weren't. His plans didn't include swinging by the house to find out.

Brian checked his watch. Time was inching along until first period.

His homeroom teacher—like most in the school—had a sign-in sheet at her desk. All a student had to do was come in and write down his or her name on the sheet and then would be free to go. Unfortunately, Michael had one of the few teachers who actually made his class sit for the full twenty minutes of homeroom. It was like no one had bothered to tell him that they were graduating in two weeks and nobody cared about attendance anymore.

Brian didn't mind waiting for Michael. He enjoyed the view as he watched several male classmates make their way off school grounds. It always amazed him how well some guys could look in a pair of tight jeans. Brian himself preferred a nice pair of chinos. The casual look tended to set him apart from some of his more slovenly peers.

He waved to assorted guys and girls as they passed, using his body language to keep them at a distance. It wasn't that Brian was antisocial, far from it. Brian was one of the most popular kids in school, as confirmed by his being one of the finalists for Most Popular in the yearbook. But Brian hated that his popularity came so easily. All he had to do was kick a ball into a net, and people clamored to be around him. And what fun was that?

"Hey, Brian," Andy Stark called as he rushed up to the Nova without noticing that Brian was shrugging him off. "Everyone's going to hang out at the old steel mill off Route 40. You coming?"

Brian didn't share Andy's excitement over spending the day at an abandoned factory getting drunk off whatever beer some kids had swiped from the local distributors. Even though his Irish heritage was supposed to make him more amenable to the beverage, he wasn't much of a beer drinker. Besides, getting drunk first thing in the morning was rather juvenile, and Brian Kinney was anything but juvenile.

"I'm waiting for Mikey," Brian replied as his eyes slowly looked up and down the boy. Andy was one of the smartest kids in their school, but did a pretty good job at keeping himself from looking like a geek. His clothes were a little too big, but Brian could tell that he had put some effort into his wardrobe. His light brown hair was a little too messy, but it had potential. At least the glasses he wore framed his face perfectly.

"I figured," Andy replied. "I meant, are the two of you coming?"

Brian had pretty good gaydar. He had always suspected that Andy played for the same team as Michael and himself. Andy also seemed to be one of the few people more interested in a friendship with Michael than Brian.

"Would you like it if Mikey *came?*" Brian asked with full emphasis on the last word.

Andy looked more confused by the question than uncomfortable with it. The kid probably didn't even realize why he was so interested in knowing if Michael was going to the steel mill or not.

Not every teenage boy was as secure in his sexuality as Brian Kinney.

"I just thought we could all hang," Andy replied.

"Maybe," Brian said noncommittally. He never liked to be tied down by other people's plans. However, the idea of being literally tied down did intrigue him a bit.

"Well, then maybe I'll see you later." Andy's slight smile failed to mask his excitement.

Brian kind of liked that someone was excited by the prospect of spending time with Michael. Of course, he didn't *love* the idea, but he pushed the unwanted feelings of jealousy aside. It wasn't that Brian had sexual feelings toward his best friend. Michael was certainly attractive enough, although it seemed he did whatever he could to cover up his looks. It was just that in many cases sex led to more complicated relationships. For Brian, sex was purely recreational. He usually ignored intimacy with the guys in his sexual life, and that was exactly why he never intended to let sex get in the way of his friendship with Michael.

Still, he was protective of Michael and didn't want him

going off on his own with just anyone, or at least, that's what he told himself. Michael tended to romanticize relationships. Brian feared that Andy was probably the same way. If the two of them got together, Brian was concerned that his friend would never truly understand the power of a purely sexual relationship.

It was an interesting proposition nonetheless.

Andy turned and crossed the parking lot in the direction of his own car. His poorly fitting baggy jeans gave no view of the tight little ass Brian expected to be underneath.

The bell rang, signifying the end of homeroom. It would take Michael about two minutes to reach the Nova. Brian got inside and started the engine. He wanted to ditch school as soon as Michael got in the car.

The radio kicked in and heads turned as Quiet Riot's "Cum On Feel the Noize" blared throughout the parking lot. That was the one problem with the Nova: the radio only picked up AM.

In Pittsburgh, the only AM worth listening to played the most incredibly heterosexual music. But any music was better than sitting in silence, and he made sure everyone in a two-block vicinity could hear his tunes.

He liked it that everyone was looking at him.

Brian closed his eyes and leaned back into the seat. He would ask Jake Thompson to look at the car one more time before graduation. Jake was Brian's "personal" mechanic. In fact, he was the whole reason Brian had the Nova in the first place.

The car had been sitting at the Mobile on Fifth Avenue back in the fall. It had a sign listing it at $1,000—a price that Brian could afford. Even better, he could afford it without having to ask his dad for help. The car was a steal largely because it had a rather sorry excuse for an engine. Brian had made a deal with Jake to fix up the engine in auto shop after school. In addition to Jake's getting extra credit for the work, Brian had arranged for a special kind of payment plan.

Blow jobs were like commerce to Brian Kinney. He would use them, on occasion, in exchange for things that he wanted. The added bonus was that Brian loved sex in any form, and he considered it a win/win scenario. He would have fooled around with Jake without any strings attached, but Brian felt it was always better to get something else for himself in the process. Of course, Jake always insisted he was straight. Brian found it a difficult argument to make, considering that most of the protesting came moments after Jake had cum in Brian's mouth.

"A little loud?" Michael yelled as he hopped in the passenger side.

"So I'm told." Brian started driving even before Michael pulled the door shut. The Nova nearly hit another car as a classmate cautiously backed out of a spot.

"Fuckin' asshole!" Missy Caldwell yelled from her dad's old BMW. That was one brand of car that Brian *was* familiar with. He could hear the laughter under Missy's anger. Her family could afford better than public school, but she always complained about how boring the kids at private school had been. If Brian had actually hit her car, she wouldn't have thought twice about the damage.

"Later Miss!" Brian yelled back to her, although he knew she couldn't hear anything over his radio.

"Did you vote?" Michael asked as he held on to the door. The Nova didn't have seat belts.

"For what?" Brian pulled out onto the street without bothering to slow down. Horns blared around him, but he ignored the noise. The Nova really didn't take to braking very well.

"For prom king and queen. Voting was this morning."

"Is that what those sheets on Mrs. Cooper's desk were for?" Brian asked honestly. "I just signed in and left. Why would I care about voting?"

"Maybe because you're up for king."

"Please tell me you didn't vote for me."

Michael's silence gave him the answer.

"Mikey, I spent the last two weeks telling everyone *not* to vote for me. It's a stupid popularity contest just like homecoming. I have no intention of wearing some cardboard crown and dancing with Missy Caldwell while everyone stands in a circle and watches. Why the hell would you vote for me?"

"I thought you were just being modest." The look on Michael's face indicated that he realized how stupid that sounded.

Brian laughed. He really couldn't fault Michael. His

friend thought he was doing something nice. "Well, I'm sure one vote won't push me over the top."

"Where are we going?" Michael turned the sound down to a more manageable level.

"Andy said something about the steel mill." Brian checked out of the corner of his eye for a reaction from Michael. There was none. "He seemed particularly interested in seeing you there."

"Why?" Michael asked honestly.

"Don't tell me you don't know that Andy likes you?" Brian asked with mock surprise. "He's been trying to get into your pants since junior year."

"Andy's gay?"

"Isn't it obvious?"

"When did you become such an expert?"

"Consider it a natural talent." Brian drove through a stop sign.

"And to think, some people are born to heal or to teach."

"Oh, I can teach you a few things. And I've been known to heal some serious aches."

After several high-speed turns and couple blown red lights, Brian pulled the Nova in front of Buzzy's Comics. The store was empty, but Brian knew it was open. The owner liked to come in early on Fridays so he could leave early as well. It bothered Brian more than a little that he knew that.

"What are we doing here?" Michael asked, getting out

of the car, not exactly sounding disappointed. "Are we going to wear comic books tonight?"

"The mall doesn't open for a half hour. I couldn't think of a better way to kill time."

That was a lie. Several ideas had sprung to Brian's mind as they were pulling out of the school parking lot. Most of them had to do with sex in some form, but he really wanted to save up for tonight. The comic book store was always a good backup plan, especially if he was going to force Michael to go clothes shopping with him. Besides, Brian liked to let Michael indulge in his one real passion.

"Hello, Michael," Buzzy said as they walked in the door. "Hello, Michael's friend."

Brian smiled as he greeted the owner. This was the only place outside of the Novotny home where he was "Michael's friend" instead of the other way around.

"I got the latest installment of Marvel's *Atlantis Attacks* crossover," Buzzy said. "You interested?"

"Nah," Michael replied, making his way to the new-releases wall. "It's not as good as *Evolutionary War.*"

While Michael and Buzzy discussed the finer points of the comic book crossover series, Brian flipped through one of the old *Teenage Mutant Ninja Turtles* comic books, from before they had sold out and become trite children's fodder. Brian hated how more and more edgier works were being homogenized for mass consumption. *Pee-wee's Playhouse* had done the same thing when it went from racy comedy sketch to Saturday-morning fare.

Buzzy didn't normally like nonregulars looking through the books, but since Brian came in often enough with Michael, the owner never said anything. The only comic books Brian ever bought were gifts for his friend. He had outgrown them a while ago, but still feigned interest for Michael's sake. By the time he finished reading the *Turtles* issue, Michael had an armful of comics and his conversation with Buzzy had switched to talk about a new star of the *Superboy* TV series.

"The mall should be open by now," Brian said, putting down the comic book.

"I'm ready." Michael was making his purchases.

"Did you leave comic books for anyone else?" Brian asked, looking over the pile.

"Plenty. There's a whole bunch of *Archie* comics and *Casper the Friendly Ghost.*"

"Who buys that crap anyway?"

"You'd be surprised," Buzzy replied.

Michael returned with Brian to the Nova. In a few minutes, they were at Westmoreland Mall, finding a spot right outside Sears. Brian hurried them through that store and out into the mall without bothering to look at clothes. He hadn't shopped at Sears since he'd realized that only blue-collar families would buy clothing at a place that also sold table saws and refrigerators. Granted, he was part of a blue-collar family, but with white-collar tastes. Brian also avoided all the crappy little shops and went straight for the men's section of Macy's. It was really only a step up from Sears, but their limited designer section would have to do.

"You're not getting a suit?" Michael asked.

"It's not that kind of club. I just want something a little nicer than chinos."

"Can I help you with anything?" an elderly woman with a raspy voice asked. She spoke with an overly forced pleasant attitude that her body language did not match. She looked as if she'd much rather be out having a smoke than be in the store helping customers.

"No thanks," Brian said, continuing through the racks toward the pants. He ignored the woman as she went off to accost another customer. "This is the men's department. You'd think they'd have some hot men working here to help out."

"What exactly do you think they're selling?" Michael asked lightly.

"Sex, Mikey. They're selling sex. Men come here because they want to look good. They want to be told that they look good by a hot woman . . . by an attractive man. That's how the store makes the sale. Some dour old biddy is not going to push any merchandise in this section."

"Brian, not everything is about sex," Michael said, browsing the racks.

"The hell it isn't. Look over there at the underwear section. See all the pictures of hot guys on the boxes? Do you think they would sell as much if they just hung the underwear on a hanger?"

"Who buys underwear off a hanger?"

"And why do they put it in a box?" Brian asked right back. "They do it to make the underwear look good. To make the buyer want to look like the guy wearing the underwear in the picture when, in fact, most guys that buy those things don't even look as good as you or me."

"So every guy that buys that underwear is gay?" Michael asked skeptically.

"No, every man that buys that underwear wants to have sex. Gay. Straight. It's all the same. Now, class is over. We're here on a mission."

"I'll alert Captain Astro." Michael said.

Brian ignored the comment as he focused on a rack of black pants, searching for a size twenty-nine waist. He found them mixed in with the thirties. "Wait here, I'm going to try these on."

Brian took his time in the dressing room determining that the pants just didn't have the right fit. It was never just a matter of slipping them on and seeing how they felt. His entire body was under consideration before a purchase was made. This pair bunched up a little too much at the ankles. He took them back to the rack and picked up several more styles.

Michael was beginning to look bored by it all.

"Why don't you get something?" Brian asked. "An outfit that makes you look even more sexy than you do leaning on that rack in those baggy clothes."

"I have plenty of things to wear tonight," Michael

replied defensively. "Are you going to be much longer?"

"Fine." Brian didn't want to press the issue, knowing that money was tight in the Novotny home. "Why don't you start pulling me some shirts? You've got pretty good taste."

"Thanks," Michael said without sounding as if he meant it.

Shopping was just one of the interests that Brian and Michael did not have in common. He couldn't get it through Michael's head that image mattered, but he didn't intend to beat the issue to death. Michael would come around eventually.

By the third pair, Brian found just what he was looking for. They were just tight enough to emphasize the things that needed to be pointed out while still being comfortable enough to breathe.

"I got some shirts," Michael said from the other side of the dressing room door.

Brian opened the door, shirtless, and couldn't help but notice that Michael appreciated the view.

Most men did.

Michael was holding up a blue-and-white striped shirt with a big red Hobie label splashed across the chest in what felt like molded rubber. He was smiling. "I think it's you. Not too flashy, not too subtle."

"Very funny." Brian reached past the shirt and grabbed the real pile in Michael's other hand. He left the door open as he went through the options. His friend hadn't let him down. There were several good choices from button-down long-sleeves to high-quality T-shirts that Michael had had the foresight to choose one size too small. Brian dropped everything on the floor when he settled on a gray T-shirt made of a cotton/Lycra blend. He pulled it on over his head. It hugged his body perfectly.

Brian looked good. Interestingly enough, the bracelet Michael had gotten him went with the outfit perfectly, as if it were meant to be. Even if it hadn't worked, Brian suspected that he would have kept it on. There was something about the bracelet that he liked, but he wasn't sure what. It wasn't exactly his style.

"Looks like we have a winner," he said, continuing to admire his body.

He had found the outfit that would get him laid.

Not that he needed to rely on his clothes to do the job for him.

chapter four

"Look at that!" Michael said excitedly. A pair of men were leaning up against a streetlight making out right on the street.

"Stop pointing," Brian said, trying to maintain his veneer of casual indifference as he pushed the Nova through the stop-and-go traffic of Liberty Avenue. "You look like a tourist."

"Oh, like you've ever seen guys kissing like *that* outside of a porn video."

Brian smiled. If he hadn't spent years cultivating his detached attitude, he would probably be just as giddy as Michael as they inched their way down the street. They were both sight-seeing, and the sights were amazing.

The sidewalks were packed with men.

These were not high school boys—well, some of them

probably were. But the overwhelming majority of them were men. Gay men. And they came in all shapes and sizes. They were young. They were old. They were hot. Whether dressed in tight clothes or wearing very little, they were everything Brian had imagined.

Liberty Avenue was unlike any place he had ever been before. Sure, Brian had driven down the stretch of road many times during the day, but it was entirely different at night. The bars were all open with music and men spilling out into the street. Several couples and even trios were making out openly; not just the ones Michael had pointed out by the lamppost. There was a sense of openness that Brian had never felt before. It was a far cry from the oppressive house he had grown up in. If he had known about this strange world earlier, he wouldn't have wasted his teen years in the school locker room and the locked bedrooms of assorted high school parties while parents were away.

"I should have worn a T-shirt," Michael said with regret. He was wearing a button-down, tan, denim shirt with blue jeans. The overall look was not entirely unappealing, but it certainly didn't show off his assets.

"That's what I told you." Brian pushed past a VW and into a parking spot at the corner of Liberty and Barkers.

"No," Michael said defensively, "you told me to change."

"Out of the blue T-shirt with the Superman logo emblazoned across the chest. I said a tight white T-shirt would be fine."

"I don't look good in—"

"We're here." Brian threw the car in park and stepped out onto the street. He smoothed down his new Hugo Boss pants and crossed around the car. As soon as he was on the curb, the throng of men surrounded him and swept him up in their motion. He grabbed Michael by the hand to make sure they didn't get separated and felt several other hands feeling him up.

And this was all happening right out in the open.

From what little Brian knew about gay Pittsburgh, he was fairly certain that the excitement of Liberty Avenue was a more recent development. Only within the last year had he started to notice the rainbow flags in a few shop windows along the drag. At first, he hadn't known what they stood for and actually thought they looked rather stupid. Rainbows were the stuff of Care-Bears and Strawberry Shortcake. His sister had filled her room with every rainbow piece of crap she could buy when she was younger. But these rainbows, he learned, were different.

They were the official flag of a world where he planned to be president someday . . . or at least dictator.

It was like Pittsburgh was coming out of the closet.

A gaggle of drag queens surrounded the boys and moved between them. Brian was forced to let go of Michael's hand and lost sight of his friend as sequins and feathers obstructed his view.

"Oh, honey, look what we have here," an extremely tall, blond "girl" said as she grabbed a piece of Brian's ass. "Fresh meat."

"Just like I like it," her friend who bore a striking resemblance to Cher replied. Her hand brushed against his cheek. "Young tenderloin."

Brian slipped through the pack and found Michael on the other side. They both took one look at each other and burst out laughing. They didn't even need to comment on it. Each of them knew exactly what the other was thinking.

Brian continued to take in all the sights and sounds as he pulled Michael through the crowd. Most of the stores were still open even though it was well after ten o'clock. People were going in and out of doorways of the shops, bars, and even a diner. The bars had names like The Ranch, Triangle, and Numbers, and one named Hepburn's looked to be frequented mostly by women. But the building on the corner with no sign on it intrigued him the most.

The windows were painted black and there was really no way to tell what was going on inside. Most of the men entering seemed to be doing so in a rather hurried manner, while the men exiting all seemed to have the same look of contentment on their face. He wanted to know about this strange place that didn't need to advertise itself. But that was for another night.

Tonight, he had another objective.

He saw the line before he saw the club.

"Holy shit," Michael said, seeing it.

It looked to be at least one hundred men deep with more filing in at the end.

At the front of the long line, Brian saw the sign welcoming him into the new world.

BABYLON.

He remembered from history class that the word came from an ancient city known for its great luxury as well as corruption. It sounded like his kind of place. But more important, it was the first time he had ever found a use for any piece of information he had learned in history class.

Brian tended to look to the future rather than to dwell on the past.

"We're going to be stuck outside all night waiting," Michael said in resignation.

"Like hell we are." Brian quickened his step without bothering to confirm whether his friend was following. He knew that Michael was.

Every head turned as Brian confidently strolled past the dozens of men in line. He didn't blame them. He looked good in his outfit. But he knew that wouldn't get him inside.

Brian slowly lifted the shirt as he passed the men. He raised it inch by inch as if giving a tantalizing strip show to the poor guys stuck in line. By the time he reached the doorman, the shirt had come off entirely. He motioned for Michael to do the same, but suspected that his friend wouldn't take part in the exhibitionism.

He was right.

It didn't matter though. Michael was with *him*.

Brian put his left arm around his friend and stuck his right hand in his own pants pocket. He gave himself a few strokes to make his tight pants look all the more appealing under his naked torso. The doorman was so busy with the line that he didn't notice.

"How long's the wait?" he asked the doorman.

"Long," the man replied without bothering to turn.

It wasn't exactly the answer Brian had been looking for. For his plan to work, the doorman had to see what Brian was offering. He tried again, throwing his hand onto the shoulder of the doorman and giving a gentle tug. "Let's do this one more time. How long's the wait?"

The doorman turned and was clearly about to make a rude comment when his gaze hit Brian's bare chest. A smile came to the man's face that grew larger as he looked up and down Brian's body, pausing for a moment at the swollen package. Brian watched as the doorman's eyes drifted over to Michael.

They lingered for a moment on him too.

"No wait at all," the man said, undoing the rope to let them in. He grabbed ahold of Brian's ass as they passed. Brian didn't mind at all. He did notice that no one in line was complaining that he and Michael had just cut in front of what was plainly an hour's long wait at least.

It was clear to everyone that Brian belonged in Babylon.

"He didn't even check our ID," Michael said in an excited whisper as they crossed the threshold.

"Because he knows that young guys like us are the reason men are going to come to this club." Brian dropped his shirt on the floor. He knew that he wouldn't be needing it.

A remix of "Like a Virgin" pounded out of the speakers louder than any music Brian had ever heard before. Such a fitting welcome. Brian hadn't been a virgin for years, but he certainly felt like one tonight.

The club was huge. Brian had assumed that the long line reflected that the place just wasn't large enough to hold a crowd. He was wrong. The place was twice the size of the school gym and was filled with more sweaty male bodies than he had seen at soccer camp two summers ago. It was like the entire gay population of western Pennsylvania had turned out for the opening.

Gay nightlife had finally come to Pittsburgh, and on Brian Kinney's eighteenth birthday, no less.

"And I thought it was wild outside," Michael said.

"This is fucking amazing," Brian said with barely contained enthusiasm.

"Emphasis on the fucking."

Men were hooking up all over the place. On the street they were at least being somewhat discreet, but apparently everyone left their inhibitions at the door—probably about the same place Brian had dropped his shirt. Men in various states of undress were dry humping to the music, riding each other much in the way Madonna rode the stage while wearing the wedding dress during her now infamous display at the MTV Video Music Awards.

Michael still looked overwhelmed by it all, causing

Brian to laugh. He secretly understood the feeling a bit as well.

"Let's get a drink," he suggested as he led the way to the bar. It would help calm Michael's and his own nerves as well. Not that he would ever let them show.

Brian had to push his way through the crowd to reach the packed bar. He couldn't help but notice that he and Michael received several glances from interested men as they passed. He didn't want to rush things, though. A drink first, then some dancing. And then who knows what could happen.

A trio of topless bartenders were pouring drinks as quickly as they could take the orders, each with the same stressed look on his face. Obviously they hadn't expected opening night to be such a huge success.

Brian didn't have to wait long to catch the nearest bartender's eye.

"Long Island Iced Tea," Brian ordered, then turned to his left. "Mikey?"

Michael halted for a moment, looking over the dozens of bottles. "Rum and Coke."

The bartender gave one last glance at Brian before turning to get the drinks. The man bent lower than any good bartender should need to and retrieved a bottle out of the cabinet. Brian and Michael enjoyed the view.

As the bartender poured the drinks, Brian caught Michael still staring at the man's naked torso.

"Snap out of it," Brian said, pulling his buddy into his body.

"Never in my wildest dreams . . ."

"I know. Isn't it great!"

Brian accepted his drink from the bartender. He held the man's gaze for a moment before turning back to the dance floor. Since the bartender had given a good view of his ass, Brian felt it was his duty to return the favor.

And that's when he saw them.

Go-go boys.

Young men—probably only slighter older than himself—dancing on platforms in their skimpy underwear. Their bodies glistened with a mixture of body oil and sweat while they moved to the music with almost pornographic maneuvers. Their full cocks were straining to get out of their G-strings.

Brian nudged Michael, but his friend was already entranced. Michael was staring with the first smile on his face that Brian had seen since they'd entered the club.

"I *love* this place!" Brian yelled over the music.

He downed his drink in one gulp and pulled Michael toward the dance floor, forcing him to abandon the rum and Coke after only a sip.

Brian felt the beat of the music pulsing through him as he made his way through the crowd. The temperature rose noticeably as he and Michael moved onto the dance floor. Hot and sweaty male bodies surrounded them as Brian pushed his way closer to the dancing boys on their pedestals. They were certainly hot to look at, but Brian had no real interest in them as conquests. It seemed too easy.

The money hanging out of their underwear was an interesting concept, though.

And he did like being near such open sexuality.

He also liked the idea of possibly taking some attention away from the mostly naked men.

It didn't take long for Brian to realize that many eyes were on him. Michael was getting a fair amount of attention as well. He shared a few glances with the men around him, but his eyes kept darting back to Brian.

"I think we're going to have some fun tonight," Brian said over the din.

"I already am," Michael replied with his sweetly innocent smile.

Brian threw his arms around his friend, pressing his bare torso up to Michael's still covered chest. He ground his crotch into his friend's. There was definite stiffening inside the jeans and his own pants as well. The maneuver wasn't solely for their pleasure, although Brian enjoyed it a bit more than he'd suspected he would. It was actually intended for the audience watching.

A guy standing behind Michael caught Brian's eye. He looked to be in his early twenties.

Blond. Shirtless. Horny.

Brian responded to the man's glare by bending at the knees and dropping Michael down a little lower for a deeper grind. The look on Brian's face was quite welcoming. The look on the stranger's face was quite interested.

"What are you doing?" Michael asked in Brian's ear.

"Flirting," Brian responded as he stood upright and pulled himself away from Michael.

The blond's head jerked to the right, then his body followed.

"I'll be back," Brian said as he left his friend to follow the guy.

Brian's eyes locked onto the muscled back of his new friend as he navigated his way through the crowd. The rest of the room faded into the music as he focused on his potential conquest. At first, he assumed the blond was leading him to the bathroom where they could have the privacy of a locked stall. Brian wasn't big on public-rest-room sex, but it would do in a pinch. However, the blond surprised him by passing the staircase that led to the bathroom.

Brian had no intention of going home with the strange man. He had heard enough stories about the stupidity of such a maneuver. But it didn't appear that they were heading to the exit either.

The blond moved into a dimly lit room.

Brian followed.

The first thing Brian noticed as he entered the darkened room was the smell. It was sex. By the moans and groans accompanying the smell, it was a lot of sex. When his eyes adjusted to the lack of light, Brian was met with a sight unlike any he had ever seen.

The undulating bodies of men surrounded him. Clothing was dropped carelessly about the room. Men were on their knees and on their backs with other men on top of them and beneath them. They were pressed up against each other in pairs and trios.

It was literally his dream come true.

The blond continued through the room until he found an empty spot in a corner. The wall butted up to a ledge, making a nice little semiprivate area. The blond turned and leaned his back against the wall. It was the first time he had looked at Brian since they had left the dance floor.

The dozens of nude men surrounding them disappeared as Brian focused on the muscular blond standing in front of him. Brian pushed his entire body onto the man. Tongues explored mouths while hands explored bodies. Brian liked what he felt. He grabbed hold of the blond's hard cock through his jeans and gave a squeeze.

A moan came out as his reward.

"Suck it," the blond begged.

Brian looked over to the conveniently placed ledge. It was the perfect height. The designers had obviously put a lot of thought into the place. He took hold of the blond under his arms and lifted the man onto the ledge.

"Do it," the blond said as if Brian needed any verbal prodding.

Brian slid his hands up the blond's thighs to the button of his Guess? jeans. The guy wasn't wearing a belt. Brian assumed that it was a way to ensure easier access. He gladly took the invitation, popping the button and slowly undoing the zipper. He could feel the hardened flesh against the back of his hand.

The guy wasn't wearing underwear either.

The blond put his arms on Brian's shoulders. He leveraged his weight against Brian's body and lifted his ass off the ledge, giving silent permission to pull off the jeans. Once Brian had the jeans around the man's ankles, he took hold of the exposed cock and began to stroke.

Brian engulfed it in one fluid motion.

The blond let out a gasp that implied that he was pleasantly surprised by the well-practiced mouth.

Brian let the cock slowly slide out from his throat and mouth until the tip rested just between his lips. Then he went to town.

The blond's hands rubbed up and down Brian's bare back. His cock filled Brian's mouth. There was nothing romantic about it. There was nothing sweet. They were having fun.

A lot of fun.

Before long, Brian felt another pair of hands caressing him as well. Someone had come to join the fun. Brian was too busy concentrating on the blond to look behind him to see the identity of the owner of the crotch that was pressed up against his ass. A quick glance above told him what he wanted to know. The blond was visibly hot for the guy behind him. That was all Brian needed to know about the new man.

The second pair of hands moved around Brian's body to the front of his brand-new pants. He did not protest as the hands worked the button and the zipper. His pants and underwear were dispatched soon enough. For the first time he was naked in a public place with a group of attractive strangers. Somehow he knew that it would not be the last.

A tongue was placed against his ass.

Brian was in heaven.

Out of the corner of his eye, Brian saw a man wearing only a jockstrap slide between him and the corner wall. Another playmate had come to join them. This one reached under Brian's bent torso. The new guy found Brian's nipples and tugged at them playfully. With so many moans in their corner of heaven, Brian wasn't sure which ones belonged to him. The guy in the jockstrap slid down the wall and under Brian's body.

One mouth sucked on Brian's cock.

One tongue licked at Brian's ass.

One cock fucked Brian's mouth.

Brian caught a glimpse of the hand belonging to the guy behind him. It was reaching into a bowl of foil-wrapped condoms at the edge of the ledge. It grabbed a small packet of lube conveniently placed beside the condoms. A moment later both the empty foil pack and the spent packet were on the floor between Brian's feet.

He braced himself.

It was going to be a very happy birthday.

chapter five

Michael leaned over his freshly ordered rum and Coke with both his elbows on the bar. He could feel the men staring at him. It was a strange feeling, one that he wasn't quite sure he was ready to experience. He had never been around so many gay people before. He hadn't even been to one of his mom's PFLAG functions yet.

Duran Duran was singing.

I'm on a ride and I want to get off.

Michael shared the feeling.

The past four years of friendship with Brian had been a great help for Michael in accepting the truth about himself. Neither of the boys had formally announced their sexual preference to the world, but somehow most people knew, or, at least, suspected. But now Michael was outing himself simply by walking in the door of Babylon.

Considering that most—if not all—of the other men in the place were gay, it shouldn't have felt so uncomfortable for him. He was finally in a place where he wasn't the outsider. Everyone here shared the trait that made him feel ostracized in his everyday life. And yet he felt more out of his element than ever.

He had actually been having fun dancing in the crowd of men with Brian by his side. Brian often bolstered Michael's confidence simply by being around and made him feel secure in even the most uncomfortable situations. It was one of the main reasons they had become friends in the first place. But when Brian had disappeared into that back room, it was like a hunk of Kryptonite had landed in the center of the dance floor. Michael had immediately began to feel conspicuous and uneasy. He knew that he was being stupid; nothing had really happened that should have changed his perspective. But it wasn't long after Brian's departure that Michael had made his way back to the bar.

"You're not going to get any ass if you don't flaunt your wares," a gravelly voice said from beside Michael.

It took him a moment to realize the voice was speaking to him.

Michael turned his head to the left. An older guy who looked to be in his early fifties and dressed in clothing much too tight for him was giving Michael the once-over.

Michael hadn't seen parachute pants in years, and even then never on anyone over fifteen . . . well, except for Michael Jackson.

"Your body language," the man said. "You're cutting yourself off."

"I'll keep that in mind." Michael turned his attention back to his drink.

"Name's Bill," the man said, undaunted. "Come here often?"

Michael was about to remind Bill that it was the club's opening night, but the guy started laughing. He must have been impressed by his own joke.

"Wait, how 'bout this one?" Bill asked. "What's your sign?"

"So, this is what it's like to be hit on," Michael mumbled. "Couple hundred hot guys and I get Rip Taylor."

"What was that?" Bill asked, leaning in too closely.

"I'm waiting for my friend." Michael glanced to the room where Brian had disappeared.

"If he's back there, you might have a while to wait."

"I'll keep that in mind."

"If you want, I could take you back there," Bill offered. "We could look for him together."

The tone in Bill's voice combined with the look on his face led Michael to conclude that that was the last thing in the world he wanted. "That's okay," he politely declined.

"Or we could just go back to my place," Bill insisted, leaning even closer.

"Umm . . . no thanks." Michael stepped away from the bar, abandoning his second drink of the evening.

"Are you sure? I have—"

"There you are!" another voice said from Michael's right.

He didn't recognize the voice, but turned in the direction anyway. A strange man was looking at him. But this was a different kind of strange man from Bill. This strange man was young, well-dressed, and beautiful. Okay, so his Gap clothes put him a little on the yuppie side—or guppie, to use the correct queer slang—but that didn't matter. He was giving Michael the once-over. That was the important part.

And Michael liked the look on his face.

"I've been searching all over for you," the new guy said.

Michael figured that the stranger must have him confused with another guy. He didn't hurry to correct the mistake.

"Let's dance," the guy said as he threw his arm around Michael's shoulder and pulled him onto the dance floor.

"I think you have me confused with someone else," Michael said as they moved to the music.

"Nope. I saw the way Bill the Troll was looking at you. I figured you could use an out."

"Bill the Troll?"

"That's what everyone calls him." The guy danced a little closer and yelled to be heard over the music. "Granted, it's not a very original nickname. He goes to all the bars on the street with the same lounge-lizard act, trying to pick up young guys."

Michael looked back at the bar. He saw that Bill was drinking the remains of the abandoned rum and Coke—just a little disgusting. Even worse, upon more careful study, Michael realized that the troll was licking the rim of the glass where his own mouth had been.

That was *more* than a little disgusting.

"Sounds sad," Michael said, focusing his attention back on the man he was dancing with.

"Every now and then someone gives him a tumble. He probably gets more action than a lot of guys around town."

Michael had heard of the concept before. Brian called it a pity fuck. Neither of the boys had any intention of pursuing the idea in their lifetimes.

"I'm Max." The guy held out his hand.

"Michael." He took the offered hand. He had never shaken the hand of someone he'd been dancing with before. It seemed like such an odd move. Then again, no strange guy had ever asked him to dance before. No familiar guy had ever asked him to either.

The two of them were moving to the music rather sedately, very different from the sexual grinding Brian had forced on Michael earlier. This was like the moves he did with Lisa and other girls at school dances. And yet it was something entirely different as well. No girl he had ever danced with had made him feel the way he did dancing with Max.

"You go to school?" Max asked as they continued gyrating to the music.

"Yeah," Michael said without thinking. Then he realized that Max was probably referring to college when he had asked about school.

"I go to Carnegie Mellon," Max said. "You know it, right?"

It was a stupid question since Carnegie was one of the most notable universities within the city limits. But Michael suspected that he was supposed to act impressed by the information.

"Yeah, I know the place." Michael didn't bother to explain that he knew of it mostly because that's where his best friend was going to desert him in a couple weeks. It seemed a little early in their relationship to share anything that personal—or anything at all.

"I'm a sophomore," Max said. "My dad wanted me to go to Harvard, but I couldn't stand to go to such an obvious school."

Michael wasn't sure he understood what Max meant by an "obvious" school, but assumed that it was just a way of dropping names. He didn't bother to say anything and Max didn't seem to mind. The student from Carnegie Mellon had enough to say about his life and his school to fill up two more songs. Michael tried to imagine Brian saying the same ridiculously pompous things that Max was saying. Michael couldn't do it. No school could change Brian that much.

He hoped.

As Max talked, Michael considered his options. He wasn't really looking for a one-night stand. Brian often talked about the fun to be had with anonymous sex, but Michael wasn't sure he was interested in that. Naturally, he wasn't naive enough to think he was going to find love at some gay nightclub, but he also knew he wasn't about to hop into bed with the first man who showed some interest. It wasn't just because he was still technically a virgin. Michael didn't think he'd ever be that open sexually. Then again, if he was going to give it a try, the guy he was dancing with would be a good start.

Michael took a quick look at the body dancing in front of him. Max was going on about some school-related function and conveniently refrained from asking questions. This gave Michael more time to focus some discreet glances. Max's body was pretty hot. His clothes were just tight enough to show himself off without being obscene. His face and hair were a little too perfectly sculpted, hinting that Max followed some kind of beauty regime. But his lips were perfect. Michael imagined what it would be like to kiss them. He began to lean more toward making a move.

Michael finally tuned back into the one-sided conversation to hear Max describing his work with the Gay and Lesbian Student Union. Somehow, he made it sound as if the group were entirely his creation. In fact, he didn't stop talking about himself until George Michael started singing about wanting someone's sex.

"So what school do you go to?" Max asked. "Pitt?"

Michael considered going along with the lie that Max had created for him. It could be helpful if Michael did decide to throw caution to the wind and go somewhere with Max. But he also wanted to test out a theory. "Allegheny Community," he said.

The look on Max's face dropped ever so slightly and almost imperceptibly. Michael didn't miss it, though. It was the look he'd suspected he would get.

The same look he feared he would get from Brian someday.

That was the only question Max asked. He was too classy to end the conversation right there and then, however. He danced another dance before insisting that he give Michael his number. There was a note of finality to the request. On the bright side it did end Michael's mental debate about how far he was willing to go.

Michael did give the guy some points for the move. It would have been much easier for Max just to take Michael's number and lose it once he left the club. Giving Michael his own number meant that Max would be committed to talking to the guy from the community college if he should ever call. Of course, Michael suspected that Max was well practiced at being noncommittal toward any phone call that came in from anyone without the potential to make at least a $50,000-a-year starting salary once out of college.

Being around Brian had trained Michael to pick up on

some telltale signs, the main one being that if Max was really interested, he would have made a move on Michael right on the dance floor. Gay men tended to be more immediate about sex. And if Max had been interested in more than just sex, he wouldn't be saying good-bye so early in the evening.

But Michael still dutifully followed Max over to the bar, where shot glasses full of slips of paper and pencils waited. Max took one of each and wrote down his number. Michael dutifully took the slip of paper and stuffed it in his pocket before they said good-bye.

Max went back to the dance floor and cruised someone who was better dressed than Michael. He didn't even bother to wait until he was out of Michael's sight.

He was just another kind of troll.

Michael looked off into the direction where Brian had disappeared too numerous songs ago. There was still no sign of his friend. When Michael noticed Bill the Troll edging closer to him, he decided that he had had enough and made his way to the front door. He knew the bus that would take him back to his neighborhood stopped only a block from the club.

He passed Brian's discarded shirt as he left.

chapter six

"I can't believe you just left me there," Brian said as he pushed the barbell up and away from his body.

"I could say the same thing to you," Michael said from above him.

"I said I'd be back."

"Yeah, after you got your rocks off."

Brian couldn't help but laugh, which made lifting the weight a bit more difficult. "Got my rocks off?" He rested the barbell on the hooks of the weight bench.

"Fuck you."

They were in Brian's garage working out with the old equipment Brian's dad had bought back when his son was five. Mr. Kinney had obviously been intent on having a strapping son and not some soft little pansy to have bought the thing when Brian was so young. But Brian didn't work out to please his father—he didn't do anything to please his father. Brian liked the way working out affected his body both internally as well as externally. Of course, the weight bench didn't compare to the weight room at Susquehanna High for a number of reasons, but since school was closed on Saturdays, this was the best they could do.

Brian was dressed in a pair of black bike shorts and a gray tank. He wore nothing underneath. It was less constricting to work out that way.

Michael was wearing the same uniform he usually wore when they worked out—a baggy T-shirt and loose-fitting sweat shorts. He wore a jockstrap underneath it all. Brian knew this because he'd peeked up the leg hole when he was lying back on the weight bench while Michael spotted him. It was only fair since he knew Michael was looking at the package in Brian's tight shorts as he lay back on the bench. That's just what guys did whether they were straight or gay.

The boys switched places. Brian could see that Michael was straining against the weight, but neither of them said anything about it. That was one of the things Brian admired most about Michael; when it was just the two of them, Mikey was up to almost any challenge.

"How did you get home?" Brian asked.

"Bus. I half expected you to show up in the middle of the night."

"I made other arrangements."

"I thought you didn't go home with strange men."

"We didn't go to anyone's home. There's actually a place where guys can go just to . . . get their rocks off when the back room at Babylon just isn't enough. You and I passed it when we walked to the club."

"How quaint."

"We should go back to the club tonight."

"So we can see if your shirt made it into the lost and found?"

Brian laughed. Throwing off his shirt the moment he had walked into Babylon had seemed like a good idea at the time, but coming into the house bare-chested first thing in the morning wasn't exactly an ideal situation. At least his mother was the only one who had seen him. She didn't say anything, though. She was good at ignoring the white elephant in any room.

He would have stopped at Michael's to pick up one of the shirts that he usually left there, but he knew he wouldn't have gotten too far without a litany of questions from Debbie. That was only one of the many differences between the two mothers. In one respect he didn't mind that particular difference; in another it bothered the hell out of him that his mom didn't seem to care.

"What do you say?" Brian asked.

"I don't know. That place was kind of lame."

"Really?" Brian guided the barbell onto the hook of the weight bench for Michael. "Because I spent the last of Granny's birthday money getting us both a membership for the year."

"Fake ID and membership to a club where men have sex together in a back room. Your grandmother would be so proud to know her money's being put to good use. I want to be there when she asks what you spent the money on."

"Don't change the subject." Brian pushed for an answer as he picked up a dumbbell and sat straddling the bench facing Michael: "Are we going clubbing?"

"I have to write my article for the last issue of the paper." Michael took the other dumbbell. "The deadline's Monday and Lisa is going to be pissed if I miss it. She already wants me to turn it in tomorrow if I can."

They did their arm curls facing one another. They sat a little closer than two straight boys probably would, but this was more due to their friendship than any other reason.

"Lisa's always threatening to kill you if you don't get your shit in on time," Brian said with a smirk. "I think she'll forgive you if you're late."

"Why'd you say it like that?"

"Because Lisa likes you."

Brian could see Michael's face go red. He didn't think it was because of the exertion from the weight.

"She does not."

"Lisa likes you. Andy likes you. All you have to do is make a move on one of them. Or both of them."

"I think we both know why I'm not going to be making a move on Lisa."

"What about Andy?"

"Haven't we gotten off subject?"

"Sex is a subject that I always get off on," Brian said with a straight face.

"Whatever. I can't go tonight."

"It's a high school paper. Who gives a shit?"

Michael dropped the dumbbell onto the concrete floor. "I give a shit. Allegheny Community doesn't even have a paper. This could be the last thing I write that ever makes it into print. Sorry it's not exciting like being a soccer stud."

Brian knew that he had crossed the line. "Dude, chill. Do you mind if I go myself?"

The obvious answer was yes, but Brian knew what his friend would say.

"What do I care?"

"Thanks, Mikey." Brian switched his dumbbell to the other arm.

Michael picked his weight up and continued the work-out. "You're going to the picnic Monday, right?"

"I guess," Brian said in his usual noncommittal way.

"It's going to be fun," Michael said, returning to his usual enthusiasm. "Hanging out with everyone."

"Between the senior class picnic, prom, the year-book signing party, and graduation itself, I think we're going to be a bit sick of hanging out with everyone. Besides, I've got everyone I want to hang out with right here."

Michael was practically beaming. Brian truly meant what he said, but that reaction was the main reason Brian had thrown out the compliment in the first place.

"I can't wait for the prom," Michael said.

"It's just another dumb school-sponsored dance." Brian put down his weight and got up to stretch his muscles.

"Yeah, but we'll have fun together." Michael joined Brian in the stretching.

"We could have fun together tonight at Babylon."

"I was talking about the prom."

"Yeah," Mr. Kinney said as he came into the garage. "What the hell is going on with your prom? Still can't find a date?"

"Going out tonight?" Brian asked his dad, trying to change the subject. He got off the weight bench and took a couple steps away from his friend to allow for the proper amount of personal space for two teen boys.

"When I was your age, I could have had any girl in school," Mr. Kinney said. "Hell, I did have them. Why can't you be more like I was?"

"Oh, I can have any girl I want."

It was true. Brian could undoubtedly have most of the

female population at Susquehanna High. In fact, over the past few years he did have a couple girls just for the hell of it, but he never considered it as much fun as having the guys.

"Then why are you going to the prom with Michael here?" Mr. Kinney asked. It was more an insult than a question.

"It's because I couldn't get a date, Mr. Kinney," Michael said quickly. "Brian felt sorry for me so he decided to go stag too."

Mr. Kinney considered Michael's response for a moment. "Good to know you're listening to me," he said to his son. "A man's got to stick by his buddies. That's the only way to succeed in this world."

Brian couldn't bring himself to look at his father. The man could turn on a dime, which made it difficult to figure out what he would say next and, more important, how to avoid an explosion. Not that Brian often avoided explosions.

"So, did you at least go on a date for your birthday?" Mr. Kinney pressed on.

It was beginning to feel as if the only way Brian could get out of the conversation was to fuck a girl right in front of his dad.

"No, I—"

"Went out with Michael," his dad finished the thought. "You know, sometimes you can spend a little too much time with your buddies."

Michael looked increasingly uncomfortable in the garage. He started moving toward the driveway. "Maybe I should—"

"Stay right where you are, Mikey." Brian knew that his friend should leave, but Brian was damned if he would allow his dad to send anyone fleeing. He shot a look of daggers at the man. "This is my friend and I'll spend as much time as I want with him."

"Look, Michael," Mr. Kinney said, ignoring his son, "I've got nothing against you. I just want to see Brian out with a girl from time to time. Don't you boys know anyone you could go out with?"

"No," Brian said as he stepped back into his dad's line of vision. "Mikey and I don't know anyone. We're losers. We have no friends."

"Don't get smart with me, boy." Mr. Kinney's volume was increasing.

"Nope. Wouldn't want to do that," Brian said.

"Where the fuck did you get that mouth?" Mr. Kinney yelled.

"Gee, let me think!" Brian yelled back. He saw Michael standing off to the side. Brian wanted to stop this, but he knew from experience that once the ride started, it was hard to get off.

"I'm just looking out for my son!"

"By telling me I shouldn't hang out with my friends?"

"If you'd spend some more time with your family, I

wouldn't have to worry about what you were doing with your friends!"

"Is that what this is about?" Brian's anger matched the intensity of his father's.

"Yesterday was your eighteenth birthday and you couldn't even be bothered to stop by the house!"

"Do you want to know what I did for my birthday, Dad?" Brian was gearing up for something that his mind was screaming at him to stop. "Do you *really* want to know what I did to celebrate my very special eighteenth birthday?"

"We picked up a couple college girls," Michael said, apparently more loudly than he had intended. "Took them back to my house. My mom was working the night shift."

It was a toss-up over which of the three of them was most surprised by what Michael had just said.

"Really," Mr. Kinney said with a smile. "And you'd rather start a fight with your old man than tell him the truth."

Brian chose not to respond. He looked down at his Reeboks instead. Somehow, he was always the one who started the fights.

Funny how that happened.

Mr. Kinney grabbed his bowling ball off the shelf. "Why do you always have to be such an ass?" He walked out of the garage and got into his car.

"I guess I was just born that way," Brian responded, mainly to himself.

"No you weren't," Michael said, jumping to Brian's defense once again, even though no one was there to defend him to but himself.

Brian came back around. He didn't usually let his father get to him, but he also didn't usually have an audience outside the family for their little spats either. "Don't let Jack get to you," he told Michael. "He's the ass."

"I should be saying that to you."

"No reason. Anything Jack says rarely bothers me. And when it does, I just remember that he's going bowling and getting drunk and will probably do that every night for the rest of his life. Jack's more pathetic than anything else. As far as I'm concerned, my dad disappeared a long time ago."

"Yeah."

Brian felt a momentary flash of regret for saying that to a friend who had never had the chance to know his father. He decided to move the conversation on. "You just went up a couple dozen points in his estimation. Jack liked the part about the college girls."

"That's not why I said it."

"I know." Things were still getting a little too vulnerable for Brian. "We're going to the prom stag, but together?"

"Well, we are. How else would you say it?"

"Stag?" Brian said to Michael once he'd confirmed that the car was long gone. "More like *fag*."

"Did you really want to tell your father that way?"

Michael asked, trying to bring the conversation back to a place Brian didn't want to revisit.

"If I'm going to Babylon tonight, I'll need a shower," Brian said abruptly.

"And a new shirt," Michael added, trying for the laugh. He didn't get one.

"You can go home now, Mikey."

"Look—"

"Mikey, go home," Brian repeated softly.

He pulled the garage door shut and turned to go into the house without looking at his friend. He didn't need Michael's calm, rational demeanor. He wanted to fuck someone.

"You shouldn't get your father riled up like that," Mrs. Kinney said as soon as Brian came in through the back door. She was clipping coupons from the Saturday edition of the Sunday paper. "Half the neighborhood probably heard him yelling."

Brian prepared himself for round two. At least it would involve less yelling.

He looked in the fridge for something to eat. There was nothing. This was normal since most of what the Kinneys ate was either frozen or ordered in. Brian enjoyed the majority of his meals over at the Novotnys'.

"I was just working out." Brian pulled a glass out of the cabinet. He held it under the sink, pouring himself some cold water. "He came out there and—"

"Your father works too hard," Mrs. Kinney said sternly.

"He doesn't need your attitude on the weekends. Especially before he's going out with his friends. I'm going to have to be the one that deals with him when he comes home. You'll be out heaven knows where. Gallivanting all night long."

"Gallivanting?" Brian liked the word. It sounded fun.

"Where did you get such a mouth?"

Brian took a sip of his water and remained silent. This was the second complaint about his mouth in the past five minutes. He usually received compliments about his mouth.

"Tomorrow night we're going to have your birthday dinner. Please be sure you're here."

He remembered back to the empty refrigerator. "Are you making something?"

"We're going to Red Lobster."

Hc had to be careful not to choke on his water. Not so long ago, he believed that the Red Lobster was considered fine dining. At least, it was to his parents.

"Sounds like fun," he said halfheartedly as he left the room.

Brian finished off his water as he reached the liquor cabinet. He considered having a cocktail while he got ready to go out, but stopped himself before he reached for a bottle of Scotch. He had looted the cabinet plenty of times before, but always when Michael was around. There was something a little pathetic about drinking alone. It was too much like his dad.

"I assume you're not coming to church with me and Mom tomorrow," Brian's older sister, Claire, said as she came down the steps.

"Round three," Brian mumbled. "Claire, why don't you stay out of it, just this once?"

"I'm just saying, it wouldn't, like, kill you."

"You never know." Brian moved to the stairs. "I could burst into flames when I touch the holy water at the entrance."

"Dad was right. You are a smart-ass."

Brian wasn't surprised that she had heard the argument all the way upstairs. He wouldn't have been surprised if people from down the block came knocking to throw in their two cents. "That's not exactly what he said."

"Sorry. I could only hear part of your exchange over the sound of the TV in my room."

"You're hilarious." He started up the steps. "I guess it's easy to be that way when all you do is hide in your bedroom." He stopped halfway to the second floor. "Why did you even bother to come home from college?"

"I don't hide in my bedroom," she said defensively.

"Yes, you do." He stopped. "Whenever dad's home. Now that you've got that little fridge from your dorm room, all you need is a Porta Potti and you'd never have to come out."

"At least I'm home. At least I act like I'm part of the family. It's more than you bother to do."

"*Acting* being the operative word." He started back up the steps. "I'll be here tomorrow for our big family celebration at Red Lobster."

"Make sure that you do," she said, then sarcastically added, "Have fun tonight."

"Oh, I intend to."

chapter seven

"Mom!" Michael called out as he entered his house.

There was no reply.

"Mom?"

His mom should have been home by midafternoon. She must have gotten stuck working overtime once again. Michael knew that she hated working at the Red Robin, but she really didn't have too many other choices. She had been a waitress for all of Michael's life.

Just because she didn't answer him did not necessarily mean that she wasn't in the vicinity. Michael checked for his mom down in the basement and looked out the back window just to be sure she wasn't in the yard.

The place was empty.

A smile crossed his face as he ran upstairs to his bedroom and locked the door behind him. Between Brian's constant visits and his mom's crazy shifting schedule, it was rare that Michael had the entire place to himself on a Saturday afternoon. He liked the idea of some uninterrupted alone time in his room.

Michael turned so he could see himself in the full-length mirror attached to his door. He concentrated on his face for a moment and tried for the hundredth time to figure out whether he was handsome. He looked for the traits that he liked in other guys—nice skin, penetrating eyes, full lips. Then he realized that he was looking for the romanticized traits that his mom's soap opera characters possessed. He tried to focus on the things that made Brian so attractive to him and wondered which of those traits he possessed.

Ultimately he decided it was easier just to wait for other people to comment on his looks. If Brian was to be believed, then apparently a couple people already thought Michael was good-looking. But Brian couldn't be right. Well, maybe about Andy, but certainly not Lisa. They were just good friends. Although friends did tend to group themselves together by levels of attractiveness as well. So he was right back where he started, wondering about his looks. The whole thing made his head hurt. Besides, he was wasting precious time.

Michael removed his T-shirt. His chest was developing nicely. It wasn't along the lines of Brian's chest, but it was moving that way. Brian had only introduced him to the joys of working out during junior year. Michael wasn't much into sports or exercise even, but he liked the results. Someday he thought he might even be comfortable enough with his body to flaunt it like Brian did.

But that day wasn't here yet.

Michael's hand rubbed against his chest, feeling the newly forming muscles. He knew that he should join his friend at Babylon tonight, but he wasn't sure that he was in the mood to watch Brian go off with a stranger again. Then again, there was always the possibility that Michael could meet someone too—at least someone who was a little closer to his own age than Bill the Troll or a little less full of himself than Carnegie Mellon Max.

Brian is probably taking his shower by now.

Michael took a step back so he could see more of his body in the mirror. He wished that he was still at Brian's house and they had just finished their workout. In his mind, the exchange with Mr. Kinney had never happened. In fact, no one was home.

In his mind, Michael had never left.

"I need to get a shower," Brian says as he gets up from the weight bench. *"Why don't you join me?"*

"I don't know," Michael says coyly. *"I should be getting home."*

"This could be a onetime offer."

"I wouldn't bet on that."

Brian pulls Michael toward him into a kiss.

"Stay," Brian pleads.

His nipples went hard. Michael circled his thumb around the right one and then the left, tickling himself slightly. His hand slid against the small indentation forming between his pecs. Someday he might have hair on his chest, but at that moment he was enjoying the smooth skin under his hand.

He took that hand and slid it down to his increasingly tight stomach, pausing at the waistband of his sweat shorts.

Michael follows Brian through the house. His eyes are trained on the tight ass contained in bike shorts as they go up the steps. A dark stain of sweat lines the material between the firm globes. Brian leads him into the bathroom and closes the door, locking it.

He turns on the water, making sure that it's hot.

Steam immediately fills the room around them, but Brian's body is never lost from Michael's sight.

Michael grasped his hardening joystick through the cotton fabric of his shorts and jock as he stared at himself in the mirror. He slowly rubbed his hand against the material. The cotton warmed his dick as it gently cradled his most sensitive organ. He could feel a drop of precum forming.

"You can't shower in those things," Brian says as he removes Michael's T-shirt.

Michael mirrors the action, removing Brian's tank top. They admire each other's chest in the growing steam.

Brian slowly peels down his bike shorts as inch after inch of his stiff dick is revealed.

Michael tugged on the drawstring of his shorts, releasing the knot. Gravity pulled them to the floor. He stood posing in only his jockstrap, admiring his body. Thin wisps of hair poked out of the sides of the cotton pouch.

He turned to look at his smooth ass. The muscles back there were forming nicely as well. Michael rubbed his glutes and felt himself grow even harder. He completed his turn and looked at himself face front again.

He slowly removed the jock and took matters in hand.

Brian crosses to Michael and embraces his friend, pulling their bodies together. His naked body rubs up against Michael's shorts.

"I think these are in the way," Brian says as he tugs at the waist.

Michael removes the shorts and jock in one fluid motion and moves his body back against Brian's. Their bodies rub against each other as they kiss.

Michael took a few steps back and lowered himself onto his bed. From that position he could still see himself in the mirror. He spread his legs and worked over his dick as images continued to fill his mind.

Steam obscures every part of the bathroom as Brian breaks the embrace. With a wink, he reaches out and grabs the shower curtain, pulling it aside. He glances back at Michael and steps inside.

Michael follows.

The shower curtain is pulled shut. The water is warm. The bodies hot.

Brian lathers his hands with soap, rubbing one over the other. The bar of soap tumbles over his fingers and palms. It disappears as Brian rubs his soap-covered hands against Michael's pecs. He takes the nipples between his fingers.

Michael reenacted the fantasy motions with his left hand. His right hand continued pumping. He could feel the fluids stirring in his body.

He leaned back on the bed, ignoring the mirror. The Captain Astro sheets felt warm against his back. His body heat was rising.

Soap fills Michael's hands as he explores his friend's body. He starts with Brian's chest and slowly works his way down.

He feels Brian's hand on his dick.

"Fuck me," Brian says.

Michael was breathing rapidly. He felt the familiar sensitivity in his lower regions. He was close.

Oh, so close.

He increased the speed, tightening his grip.

"Fuck me, Mikey," Brian begs. "Fuck me."

Michael's hand was a blur.

Brian turns and leans forward, presenting a welcoming target.

His moans echoed through the room, secure in the knowledge that he was alone.

Michael takes aim with his dick and rams it home.

Cum shot over his body in several squirts that landed

on his stomach and chest. One shot even reached his lips. He flicked out his tongue and tasted his own juices.

He continued to milk his dick as his breathing returned to normal.

"Michael!" his mom yelled as the front door slammed. "Get your butt down here!"

"Oh, shit," he said to himself in an agitated whisper as he sprang into action. "Just a minute!" he yelled downstairs.

Michael grabbed for his box of tissues, but remembered that he had used it up the other day while fantasizing about Brian and himself in the backseat of the Nova. He looked around the room for a towel or something. All he could see were comic books, and he wasn't going to ruin any of those. He grabbed for the T-shirt he had worn to work out in and rubbed it against his body, hoping it would pick up the errant fluids, making sure to get his chin too. He spent some additional time working the shirt over his hands.

They were a mess.

Once Michael confirmed that he had gotten up as much as he could, he threw his jock and shorts back on and riffled through his drawers for a clean shirt. After what felt like forever, he hurried down the stairs and tried not to get too close to his mom for fear of any lingering scents tipping her off.

"Reading your comic books again?" she asked with a laugh.

He blushed when he realized that she knew what he was doing upstairs.

"How was work?" He suspected that the question would shift her off topic.

"That asshole Mulcahey." Michael's mom had referred to her boss as "that asshole Mulcahey" so many times that Michael was beginning to think That Asshole was the guy's first name. "He made me stay late to help seat the dinner crowd. It's a diner for crying out loud! First come, first serve!"

"You should totally quit." Michael tried to make his way into the kitchen. He could still feel dried cum on his hands and wanted to give them a thorough washing.

"If only we didn't have to eat. Or you didn't have to go to college."

"I was thinking I could help out at the diner again this summer."

"I'm sure you could find something better. Besides, whatever you make is your money. You're going to need it next year for books and going out."

"Yeah, but—"

"I was thinking it's about time to put up the screen doors," Debbie said, changing the subject. "The weather's been getting warmer. Can you help me out before it gets dark?"

The phone rang.

"No problem," Michael said as Debbie answered the phone.

Her face fell into a serious expression that Michael did not usually see.

"Hold on," she said into the phone before handing the receiver to her son. "Say hi to Vic while I get the phone upstairs."

Debbie had been taking all of her calls from her brother upstairs lately. These calls usually coincided with the serious expression she was wearing more and more often. Michael wondered what was going on.

"Hi, Uncle Vic."

"Hey, Michael," Vic replied excitedly. He always sounded happy when he spoke with his nephew. Lately, he had been sounding a little too happy. "How's the high school graduate?"

"Haven't graduated yet, but soon. Can you still come down for the ceremony?"

"Wouldn't miss it for the world."

Michael was really close to his uncle, even though Vic did live six hours away in New York. They also had a lot in common. Well, one thing in common primarily.

They were both gay.

"I was thinking of visiting you this summer," Michael said.

"That sounds wonderful."

"We'll see about that." Debbie had picked up the extension in her room. "Maybe we can both go."

"Deb, how am I supposed to take my nephew to all the good clubs with his mom tagging along?" Vic asked with a laugh.

Debbie, however, was not laughing. "Michael, go bring

the screens up from the basement while I talk to your uncle."

"Sure, Mom. Bye, Uncle Vic."

"Talk to you later."

Michael hung up the phone and went over to the sink to wash his hands. When he reached for the soap, he couldn't help but flash back to his fantasy shower with Brian. It was only a momentary recollection since his mind was also occupied by the phone conversation that was taking place between his mom and his uncle. She usually played along when Vic would joke with Michael like that. The lighthearted—and often off-color—sense of humor was both the best and worst part of having her for a mom. Michael tried to put the nagging questions out of his mind as he brought up the screens for the front and back doors.

"Okay, Michael, let's get to work," Debbie said as she came back down the stairs ten minutes later. She had changed out of her work uniform and into jeans and a T-shirt with a red puff painting of a peace sign she had done herself. Her eyes were red and puffy like the shirt.

"Is everything okay?"

"Fine," she said in an obviously manufactured cheerful voice. "I just miss him."

Michael knew that his mom was lying, but he also knew that she would tell him what was going on when she was ready. The two of them had an open and honest relationship. If something were really wrong, she would have said something by now.

At least, that's what he told himself.

"Help me with this door, honey," Debbie said as she pulled at the clasps on the plastic window in the front door.

Changing the screens was an annual ritual they had started back when Michael was a still a child. By the time he was ten, Michael had realized that it was really a one-person job, but for some reason Debbie made it into an event every year. She tended to do that with a lot of things in life. A couple of years later Michael concluded that she did these things to make up for his having grown up without a father.

John Novotny had died in a jeep accident in Vietnam only two weeks after his son was born. Aside from a shrine Debbie had created over the mantel, the only thing Michael had that had belonged to his father was the Swiss Army knife he kept in his room. He generally used it to open the packages his action figures came in.

And for those rare blood-brother ritual bonds, of course.

Michael figured that the little mother/son traditions were just her way of showing that they would always be there for each other from the big events to the simple chores.

"So the prom is this week," Debbie said as they pulled the window out of the door.

"Don't say it. You know I'm going with Brian . . . as friends."

"Did I say anything?" Debbie asked with mock innocence. "I know you're not comfortable asking another boy. I was just wondering if there was some guy that you *wanted* to ask. Or if maybe some boy tried to ask you."

"Mom," Michael said in a tone that begged her to drop the subject.

Debbie rarely acknowledged that tone. "Or maybe some girl. I know my boy is breaking hearts at that school."

Michael got the screen for the door. "I didn't want to ask anyone. And no one wanted to ask me."

"I'm sure Lisa wanted to. She's a cutie. Have you ever thought about giving her a tumble? Just to be sure."

"Mom!" Michael often found himself shocked by the things that came out of his mom's mouth. He was even more surprised that she was the second person that day to suggest that Lisa had feelings for him.

"I'm just saying—"

"Well, stop." He slid the screen into place. "Lisa's just a friend. The only interest she has in me is if I get my article in to her on time."

"I doubt that."

"Why are you pushing girls on me all of the sudden? You were the one that told me I was gay."

"Sometimes a mother makes mistakes," she said with surprisingly little laughter.

"I think you called this one right, Mom."

"I'm just saying that I want you to go out and have fun

more often. Fun that isn't entirely dependent on Brian Kinney."

"What is it with parents trying to separate me and Brian today? Brian's dad said the same thing."

A look of exaggerated horror crossed Debbie's face. "Forget everything I just said. I never want to agree with anything Jack Kinney has to say."

"Mom, he's not that bad."

Debbie shot her son a skeptical look. "What's important is that you have fun. These are your last few weeks of high school. You should be living life. Just promise me you're being careful."

"I'm not really doing anything to be careful about. But I promise."

"That's my boy." She wrapped him up in a hug. "Come on, let's go do the back door."

"In a second." Michael reached for the kitchen phone. His mom had made a good point about going out and having fun. All his research was pulled together for the newspaper article. He even had the article laid out in his head already. He could easily dash it off by Sunday evening even if he did go out with Brian.

He dialed the number that he had memorized.

"Hello?" Claire answered.

Michael was relieved that he didn't have to talk to Brian's mother.

"Hi, Claire, it's Michael. Is Brian there?"

"Nope. Gone for the night."

"Oh, okay." He didn't bother to mask his disappointment. "Thanks."

Michael hung up the phone. He considered surprising Brian at Babylon but thought better of it. By the time Michael showered, changed, and hopped the bus, Brian could have already gone off with any number of men. Michael had stupidly passed up his opportunity for some fun in exchange for doing schoolwork.

He had made dumber mistakes in his life.

"The screen's not going to change itself," Debbie said from the back door.

"I'm coming," he said, shaking his head.

chapter eight

"Here we are," Brian said Monday afternoon as he turned the Nova off Beechwood Boulevard and pulled into a parking spot on the blacktop. "Prick Park."

Michael saw the joke coming from two miles away—literally. The car was about that distance from the park when he had made the connection himself: "Frick Park. Frick."

They looked at one another and said in unison, "Frick you!"

Sometimes the way their minds worked scared the both of them.

Michael reached into the backseat to get the bag of food his mom had packed for them. It was heavy and he had to strain to pull it over the back of the bench seat he was in. "Dear God, Mom made a lot."

"Someone should work out more," Brian said, getting out of the car empty-handed.

"Someone should help out more," Michael said, getting out of the car with the shopping bag full of food.

"Hey, I drove."

"Because you didn't want to take one of the school buses over," Michael reminded him as they crossed the parking lot.

"Still gets me out of lugging the food."

Michael gave up the argument that he would never win.

The Susquehanna High senior class officers had reserved one of the picnic areas of Frick Park for the annual lunch weeks in advance. They had also arranged for school buses to take the students over to the park, but allowed for anyone who wanted to drive to do so. Most of the class had taken the second option since then they wouldn't have to rely on the bus if they wanted to leave early.

Brian would have insisted on taking his car even if the bus were the only option.

A radio was playing somewhere in the park. The Beastie Boys were singing about fighting for your right to party.

Michael stood at the edge of the parking lot looking for his friends. It was going to be a difficult search. Only half of the four hundred graduating seniors had shown up for the picnic, but that was still a large group to contend with. Add to that the assorted teachers who had come and it would probably take a few minutes to locate the people he actually wanted to spend time with.

It was odd seeing his teachers in casual clothes. They did look more relaxed than he had ever seen them, although a few did look a little uncomfortable. In some cases, it was downright disgusting. Eighty-year-old home ec teachers should not be wearing short shorts, he decided. However, one teacher among the crowd certainly stood out.

"Wow," Michael said as he momentarily abandoned his search for his friends.

"Wow, what?" Brian looked in the direction Michael's head was turned. "Oh. Yeah, Gary's here."

"I never realized Mr. Palmer was so . . ."

"That he is."

Mr. Gary Palmer was in his late twenties/early thirties. Michael had never actually had him as a gym teacher, but Brian had. He was also the soccer coach and, on rare occasions, Brian's fuck buddy.

Michael knew that the gym teacher was handsome with his dusty brown hair, masculine face, and muscular body. He was one of the youngest teachers in the school and by far the hottest. It figured that Brian wouldn't have settled for less. But Mr. Palmer always wore khaki Dockers with loose-fitting Polos to school. He never went in for the sweats, shorts, or T-shirts that the rest of the gym teachers unadvisedly wore. Michael finally realized the reason why when seeing him in the shorts and tight-fitting T-shirt. If

Mr. Palmer wore more flattering outfits like that to school, every student at Susquehanna High would be after him—male and female.

"I guess I know what you'll be doing this afternoon," Michael said. "Or who."

"That wouldn't exactly be discreet now, would it?"

"Michael! Brian!" Lisa yelled, waving to them from a picnic bench conveniently positioned under a nice shade tree.

"Speaking of not being discreet," Brian added.

The yelling and waving did lack a certain subtlety, but it helped Michael locate his friends. It was also likely the reason his mom and Brian thought Lisa was interested in him. It was just her natural exuberance. She was a very excitable person. They probably just noticed that side of her when she was around Michael, but he knew she was like that all the time. It didn't mean anything.

"We saved you guys seats," Lisa said when the pair reached the table. She was wearing her Fido Dido T-shirt of the stick figure with the crazy hair. That was one trend that Michael was never going to understand.

"Thanks," Michael said as he sat on the bench, dropping his overstuffed bag onto the table.

"Looks like Mom's been at it again," Lisa commented when she saw the bag. She'd been calling Debbie Mom since elementary school. Michael did the same with Lisa's mom—but never with Brian's. "I bet there's enough food for everyone here."

"You can have my share," Brian said. "I'm on a diet."

"Whatever," Sharon Vincent said in her usual blunt manner. "Sometimes you act more like a girl than I do."

"Sometimes Rambo acts more like a girl than you do," Brian shot back.

"Fuck you," Sharon said with a laugh. Michael noticed she didn't argue the point. Probably because it wasn't that off base.

Michael was the center of attention while he unloaded a pair of sandwiches, some fruit, potato chips, potato salad, cookies, juice boxes, bottles of water, and two individually wrapped pickles. No matter how tight money got in the house, Debbie always made sure an abundance of food was on the table. It was a wonder that Michael was not a hundred pounds heavier.

Everyone was used to this kind of presentation from Michael. Most of the kids there had known him since either elementary school or junior high and had experienced the Novotny food fair before. Five students watched as Michael finished unloading the bag. Christine Walsh and her on-again, off-again boyfriend, Ian Holmes, were at the far end of the table facing each other and splitting a pizza they had picked up on the way to the park. Next were Lisa and Sharon, sitting across from each other. Each girl had her own hastily packed lunch. Andy Stark sat beside Sharon and was unusually quiet as he munched on a peanut butter and jelly sandwich.

That left three empty spots at the table.

Brian still hadn't sat by the time Michael finished emptying the bag. It seemed odd, until Michael realized that Brian was waiting for him to sit first. Then, the reasoning became clear. One empty seat was next to Andy, with two next to Lisa. The simple act of sitting down to lunch had just turned into a chess match. Brian was waiting to see which move Michael would make.

If Michael sat next to Lisa, that would leave an open spot beside him where Brian could sit.

If Michael sat next to Andy, then Brian would sit across from him and stare intently, trying to make Michael so uncomfortable that he would be forced into making a move on a guy he had no interest in.

The decision was simple. Michael sat beside Lisa and watched Brian, with his smug little smile, as he sat beside Andy. Brian slid the empty bag off the table and onto the bench beside Michael.

Brian didn't want anyone else joining them at the table.

"I loved your article," Lisa said between bites of her sandwich. "It was great how you brought up all that stuff about growing up in the eighties. I was really impressed with how you ended it by comparing our dumb little protest against banning Coke machines from the lunchroom with the uprising in Tiananmen Square."

"Yeah, that was on the news the other night," Michael explained. "It's looking like it might end pretty soon, so I figured it was good to throw something topical in."

"I liked it too," Andy chimed in, but looked suddenly

embarrassed. "Lisa let me read it. I hope you don't mind."

Brian shot Michael a look.

"Not at all," Michael said, ignoring Brian. "I wrote it to be read."

"Oh, yeah," Andy said, returning his focus to his sandwich. Andy did tend to get a little shy when Michael was around. But Michael didn't think that necessarily meant anything.

"You did spend a little more time than necessary on the fiftieth anniversary of Superman," Lisa added. "I had to cut that down a little."

"Did you finish getting the paper laid out?" Michael asked.

"I had to stay up until five this morning and nearly polished off a three-liter bottle of Mountain Dew, but it's done."

"How does the center spread look?" Christine asked. "With my piece on who's going to what colleges."

"Came out nice," Lisa said.

Christine obviously wanted more praise. "Did you think—"

"How about the year's sports recap?" Ian interrupted. "That's what I'm looking forward to." He was on the basketball team, baseball team, and ran track. But even though he played three sports, he never managed to get as much ink as Brian did for his soccer exploits—the ones that *could* be written about.

"Thanks," Christine said, throwing down her slice of pizza. "I put a lot of work into my piece. You could at least act like you care."

"And they're off," Sharon said, as if she were announcing one of the harness races at Ladbrook at the Meadows.

Christine and Ian would find any reason to start an argument. And if there wasn't a reason, one of them could be trusted to start something up anyway. No one understood why they were together, least of all them.

"Brian has a fair share of the sports page," Lisa said, trying to bring the subject back to the paper and not the lovers' spat. "No one else in the school got a full-ride sports scholarship."

For the first time, Brian looked a little uncomfortable, being in the spotlight. "So, Andy, you're kind of quiet. Did you write anything for the last issue of the paper?"

Andy took a moment to finish chewing on his sandwich. "I was busy working on my valedictory speech."

"You're valedictorian?" Michael asked, honestly excited for his friend.

"Fuckin A!" Sharon said, leading a round of congratulations. At least it stopped Christine and Ian from their bickering . . . for the moment.

"I was sure that bitch Lori Stephens was going to be number one in the class," Michael added.

"My GPA is one-tenth of a point above hers," Andy said, beaming with pride.

"Wow, cute *and* smart," Brian said, looking straight at

Michael. "You're going to make someone a perfect husband someday."

Luckily, the rest of the table joined in the conversation and pulled attention away from Brian's comment.

As they discussed their class rankings, Michael saw Brian looking over toward the Nova. Jake Thompson was standing in the parking lot looking at the car. Michael would have thought it an odd sight, but he was familiar with the routine. Brian leaned away from the table as if about to stand.

"I thought you were going to be discreet," Michael quickly whispered across the table.

Brian leaned in and whispered, "With Gary. Who gives a damn if someone sees me walking off with Jake?"

"My mistake," Michael mumbled.

"If you'll excuse me," Brian said to the group as he got up from the table. "I've got to talk to Jake about the Nova. I think it needs one last checkup before school's over. You know, look under the hood. Check the fluids."

"Got it," Michael said abruptly. He watched as Brian walked over to the parking lot. The two boys spoke for a moment, leaning against the Nova, before they made their way over to a collection of trees. Like Lisa's yelling earlier, this was not exactly a subtle move, but Michael figured he was the only one watching them.

He was wrong.

When Michael returned his attention back to the table, he noticed that Andy was giving him a questioning look.

Michael couldn't be sure what the question was, but he had a pretty good idea.

"Isn't this park beautiful?" Lisa asked.

Michael knew her well enough to know that the question was leading to something.

"Let's go for a walk," she said as she grabbed Michael's arm and pulled him up from the table.

"Okay," he said as if he had a choice.

As he looked back, he could see a look of disappointment on Andy's face. It was the first time he thought that maybe Brian was right and Andy was interested in more than friendship. Michael wasn't sure what he thought about that. He had never really given Andy a second thought in that way. Brian was right about the kid's being a good catch— smart, not too bad looking, and the kind of guy his mom would love—but something was missing. Michael just wasn't all that intcrested. There were no sparks.

"Hello?" Lisa said, tapping lightly on his head. "Earth to Michael. You in there?"

Michael snapped back to reality. "Sorry, just thinking. What were you saying?"

"I said that we were allowed to wear shorts today. Why did you wear jeans? Afraid to show your pasty white legs?"

Brian was totally wrong about Lisa, however. She had no interest in Michael beyond friendship. They had known each other for so long that he thought of her more like a sister. She certainly teased him like a sister. And she was right about the jeans.

"It's a little cool today," he said, not wanting to give her the satisfaction.

"It's going into the nineties. You're just afraid that you won't look as good in a pair of shorts as Brian does."

She called that right too. Michael tried not to think about Brian. He probably wasn't wearing his shorts anymore.

"Is my vanity that transparent?"

"Only to me," she said, then looked a little uncomfortable. "You could have worn your Jams. Then you wouldn't have shown too much leg." She playfully grabbed at his thigh.

"It just adds to the mystery," he said, pulling away.

"Oh, you're a mystery all right."

They continued their stroll around the park, talking about graduation and college while saying hi to various people they passed. It was just like most of the other talks they had had throughout their lives. Except that Lisa started to ramble on as if she was nervous about something halfway through the conversation.

"So, are you going to save me a dance at the prom?" she asked, speaking rather quickly as they came to a clearing between a circle of trees. "I mean a slow dance. I'm sure we'll be dancing as a group most of the night. For the fast songs, that is."

"Of course I have a dance for you. Maybe two," Michael said as he explored the area. "This is cool. We're like totally cut off from the rest of the park."

"It is nice. Sometimes the rest of our friends drive me

insane. Christine and Ian fighting all the time. Sharon's mouth. It's nice to get away from them."

"We'll be away from them soon enough." Michael sat down on the ground. He leaned back so he could get some sun on his face. His feet kicked at a patch of dirt. "With everyone going to different schools."

"I'm sure we'll stay in touch," she said as she joined him. "At least, I *know* you and I will. So what are your plans for the summer?"

"I was thinking of going to visit my uncle in New York."

"Cool."

"You?"

"My family might drive out to the Jersey shore for a couple weeks." She hesitated. "My mom said I could bring a friend."

"Sounds like fun. Are you going to take Sharon or Christine?"

"Actually, I was thinking—"

"There you are," Andy said, a little too loudly for the silence of the clearing. He was pushing his way through some bushes with the rest of their picnic gang following— minus Brian, that is.

"We didn't interrupt anything?" Sharon asked with a leer. "Did we?"

"What would you interrupt?" Michael asked honestly.

"Nothing," Lisa said. "She's just being Sharon."

The group joined them, sitting in a circle around the patch of dirt. The conversation flowed smoothly while

Michael wondered if this was the last time he was ever really going to spend with these friends. It seemed unlikely that most of them would keep in touch after graduation. They were close, but not that close. He shared Lisa's belief that the two of them would stay friends. In fact, he was more confident about that friendship lasting than he was about him and Brian.

"And what's going on back here?"

Think of the devil and the devil appears.

Brian came out through the bushes, finishing off the remnants of a water bottle. As he approached, he smiled at Michael, showing that he was holding a Certs mint firmly between his teeth.

As if Michael had any doubt about what Brian had been up to.

"I've got an idea," Brian said as he joined the circle and placed the empty water bottle in the center of the dirt patch. "Let's play a game."

Michael didn't need to be a genius to figure out what his friend had in mind. "Isn't spin the bottle a little juvenile for Brian Kinney? I thought you were all fired up to be an adult."

"That's the thing about Brian Kinney. He can choose to be an adult when he wants, and a child when he wants."

"And he can choose to refer to himself in the third person if he wants," Michael added.

"Must be nice living in your world," Sharon said.

"Oh, it is," Brian replied with that trademark Brian Kinney smile. "So who's in?"

"Sounds like fun to me," Christine said, mostly for Ian's benefit.

Her boyfriend jumped at the bait too.

As did Sharon.

"Michael, Lisa, and Andy seem to be the only hold-outs," Brian said. "So what do we think—"

"I'm in," Michael said, sounding none too happy about it. He preferred getting into the game instead of listening to whatever was about to come out of Brian's mouth. He was surprised that both Lisa and Andy caved so easily after he joined in.

"I'll go first," Brian said as he gave the bottle a twist.

For the first time in his life, Michael hoped that he wasn't going to have to kiss Brian.

He was saved for the moment since the bottle landed on Ian.

"Spin again," Christine said. "Until it lands on a girl."

"Not so fast," Brian replied. "What fun is it if we stick to the same boring gender rolls? I say we have to kiss whoever it lands on, male or female."

"What?" Andy asked in uncomfortable shock.

Michael couldn't be sure, but he suspected that Brian had worked some kind of magic on the bottle so it had landed exactly where he had wanted it to land. Then again, more guys than girls were in the group, so it could just have been the luck of the draw.

"I'm not going to kiss any girl," Christine said.

"I don't know," Sharon said with a gleam in her eye.

"Sounds like it could be fun." Sharon was usually the first one to go along with Brian's plans.

"Seems that the only person that matters at the moment is Ian," Brian said as he stared in the direction the bottle was pointing. "Are you afraid to kiss me?"

"I don't care," Ian said, and he leaned forward and gave Brian a fast kiss on the lips.

"Well, ladies and gentlemen," Brian said. "It looks like we have a game."

Ian spun next and the bottle landed on his girlfriend. Groans filled the clearing as everyone watched him kiss Christine. It was something the group had sat through often.

When the kiss finally ended, Christine spun and it landed on Sharon.

"Forget it," Christine said. "I quit."

"Christine, I'm hurt." Sharon pouted out her bottom lip.

"If I can kiss Brian, you can kiss Sharon," Ian said as a challenge.

Christine looked uncomfortable with the whole thing.

"We don't want to force you," Brian said. "If Sharon disgusts you so much—"

Sharon shut him up with a light smack to the head.

"It's just a game," Lisa said.

Christine had apparently worked up her courage because she closed her eyes and leaned into the circle without saying a word. Sharon leaned forward as well and their lips met. Their kiss held several seconds longer than Brian and Ian's kiss had.

"That wasn't so bad," Christine said as she leaned back.

"Thanks for the compliment," Sharon said.

"You know what I mean," Christine shot back.

"Next," Brian said, hurrying the game along.

Sharon's spin landed on Brian. Their kiss lasted a rather long time and tongues were most definitely involved. Then Brian's spin landed on Lisa. Their kiss was almost as long as the previous one, but without tongues.

Lisa spun and the bottle pointed to Michael.

He knew that he would have to kiss someone eventually. Michael was just glad it hadn't landed on Brian. No telling what kind of display Brian would have put on in the center of the circle.

"You ready?" Michael asked.

"Yes."

Michael leaned to his right and kissed his friend. He could feel her shaking as their lips met. She was also pushing against him a bit too hard, which he chalked up to a lack of experience. Neither of them had a lot of history in kissing. After a few seconds, Michael pulled away.

Silence filled the clearing.

Lisa looked a little uncomfortable.

"Keep it moving," Brian said, looking directly at his best friend.

Michael took the bottle and gave it a spin.

It landed on the person sitting to his left.

Andy.

Now Michael was sure that Brian had the bottle rigged in some magical way.

"It's about time I got to play," Andy said with a forced laugh. "Figures it would be with Michael . . . I mean—"

"Close your eyes," Christine said. "It helps."

"You know, my ego's really taking a beating today," Sharon said.

"You know what I mean."

Michael tried to think of something funny to say to lighten the mood, but he couldn't. Instead, he just closed his eyes and leaned forward. A moment later he felt Andy's lips pressing against his own.

The kiss felt considerably better than his kiss with Lisa. Their lips just seemed to melt into one another. He couldn't be sure, but he thought that he felt Andy's mouth trying to open.

Michael was caught totally off guard when he felt Andy's hand against the back of his head, pulling him deeper into the kiss. Michael didn't fight the pressure and opened his mouth slightly, hoping that Andy would get a little bolder. He totally forgot about the rest of the circle of friends as he raised his left hand and slid it to the back of Andy's head.

And felt another hand already there.

Michael's eyes shot open and he saw Brian holding on to the back of Andy's head, gently pushing him forward. Andy's eyes were closed and both of his hands were on the ground. It didn't take a genius to realize what was going on.

Michael started to pull out of the kiss, but Brian's hand held him tightly in.

Andy sensed that something was wrong and opened his eyes. A look of panic crossed his face when he realized that it wasn't Michael's hand caressing his hair.

Both boys struggled against Brian's grip for a moment until they broke free of the kiss.

"Asshole!" Michael yelled.

Various people around the circle were laughing. Some were laughing out loud, like Brian, while others, like Lisa, were laughing more softly.

Michael and Andy weren't laughing at all.

"Game over," Michael said. Brian had simply pissed him off, but it was clear that Andy had actually been hurt by the joke.

"Oh, come on," Brian said. "We were just starting to have fun."

"Well, find some other way to amuse yourself," Michael said.

"Okay," Brian said without skipping a beat. "How about a game of truth or dare?"

Michael tried not to laugh. "You're impossible."

"I know."

chapter nine

Brian reached into his closet and pulled a shoe-box off the shelf, blowing dust off the lid. He opened the box and pushed aside the tissue paper, exposing the fine Italian leather Ferragamo shoes to the light. He had saved for weeks to buy the shoes last fall. It was the first truly designer item he had ever purchased. The shoes had only been worn once, to a wedding of some cousin he hardly knew. Expensive shoes like that weren't worn every day. They were finally going to have their real debut. He closed the lid again and put the shoes into the duffel bag he had on his bed.

He checked his clock. It was already past the time he had wanted to leave. Michael was probably complaining about his being late already.

"What's with the bag?" Claire asked as she walked into Brian's room through the open door. She tended to get in his business on those rare occasions she came out of her room lately. He figured it was her way to act like a big sister getting involved in her brother's life, but it just came across as being nosy. The room thing was new, however. She used to spend more time hanging out with their parents before she left for college. Brian figured that since he was never home, she had finally given up on the whole "family unit" idea as well.

They hadn't always been this way, of course. It wasn't long ago that Brian and Claire had actually cared what each other was up to. That had all changed in recent years, but Brian had no idea what had happened. He knew it had something to do with his parents, but he could never pinpoint when things had taken a turn—not that he spent too much time trying. The days of the family going to Kennywood Park or the St. Patrick's Day parade together were long gone.

"I'm getting ready at Michael's," he casually replied as he threw his brush, cologne, and assorted hair and body products into the duffel.

"I don't get to see you in your tux?" She sat on his bed beside the bag. "I still have that picture of you with me in my prom dress."

Brian held up his wrist, considering the bracelet that Michael had given him for his birthday. It didn't really go with a tuxedo, but no one would see it under the shirt-sleeve. He left it on. "I'm sure Michael's mom will take plenty of pictures."

"That's not the same," she said, sounding only mildly disappointed. "But I get it."

"Good, because I was worried," he said in a tone that indicated otherwise. "With Mom off at the church rummage sale and Dad playing poker with his friends, I figured it wouldn't matter that I just split."

"Makes sense."

Brian threw a couple more things in the duffel and zipped it up. "Anything else?"

She didn't get off the bed. "Sorry I was such a bitch the other night."

"No problem." He assumed that she was talking about Saturday, but he had already put whatever she had said out of his mind. Other things that were said that night still remained, but Claire's participation in the grief was fairly insignificant.

"But, you know, you should really give Mom a break at least. I understand Dad, but Mom's—"

"Can you save this for some other time?" Brian grabbed the bag. "I've got to get to Michael's."

"You can't keep running away from your problems."

"First of all, I'm *ignoring* my problems. When I run away from them, you'll know it. And secondly, I'm not running anywhere. I'm going to the prom, an event that has been on my calendar for over a month. So maybe the next time you want to have a little heart-to-heart, you could choose a more appropriate time. In fact, let me know in advance and I'll make sure I'm out for the evening."

Brian left his room.

"I hope you and Michael have fun tonight," Claire called out to him, sounding as if she meant it.

"I'm sure we will," he replied without looking back.

"Where the hell is Brian?" Michael asked after checking his watch and peeking out the front window for the fourth time in the past ten minutes.

"The prom's not going anywhere," Debbie said. "Have another mozzarella stick."

"No thanks," Michael said, joining his mom and her friend Rosie in the kitchen. A smorgasbord of hors d'oeuvres covered the tabletop. It was far more than four people could ever manage to consume, especially considering that Brian was very particular about his eating habits.

Michael's mom had invited Rosie over to see the boys off to the prom. He liked to see his mom hanging out with friends. He liked it even more that Rosie was a work friend and not another PFLAG mom. His mom tended to center her life around his. It worried him that she might be lost once he moved out of the house—whenever that would be.

"They're going to have food at the prom, Deb," Rosie reminded her from her seat at the kitchen table.

"Rubber chicken and undercooked vegetables," Debbie

replied. "You'd think you'd get more for seventy-five bucks."

The doorbell rang.

"Finally." Michael tried not to look too eager as he went to open the door.

"Hey." Brian stood in the doorway with his tuxedo bag slung over his shoulder.

"It's about time." Michael took the duffel bag from Brian and put it down on the couch.

"Come in and have some food," Debbie yelled from the kitchen.

"That's okay, Deb. I'll eat —"

"Come in and have some food." Debbie and Brian had fought over food many times before. She always won.

"You don't want me to look fat in my tuxedo, do you?" Brian asked as he gave in. He draped his tuxedo bag over the back of the couch and joined everyone in the kitchen.

"You need some meat on those bones," Debbie replied. "Look at him, Ro, doesn't he look like a skeleton?"

"You are a little thin," Rosie agreed.

"Hi, Mrs. Catalano." Brian picked up some pigs in blankets. "I didn't realize we were having a party."

"You know Debbie," Rosie said. "Any reason to cook."

"Wait until you see next week's spread." Debbie took even more food out of the oven. "You're going to stop by with your parents before graduation?"

"That's the plan." Brian sounded skeptical that it would actually happen.

"We're going to be late," Michael said as he pulled Brian toward the stairs.

"Relax, Mikey. No one shows up before eight-thirty. We've got plenty of time." Brian stuffed a little piggy in his mouth.

"I thought you wanted to stop off on the way," Michael whispered.

"We've got time for that too." Brian grabbed his things.

The boys hurried upstairs to the bedroom. Michael shut the door behind him once they were inside. He went into his closet to bring out his tux while Brian laid his bags out on the bed and opened the duffel.

"This is boss," Michael said. "I've never worn a tux before."

"Me neither. Which is why I got us something special for the occasion." He pulled a small plastic bag out of the duffel.

The bag was from the Big Q discount department store. Michael knew that Brian wouldn't be seen dead at the Big Q and assumed the bag had just been lying around the house. It made him all the more curious about the contents. "What did you do now?"

"Red or blue?" Brian pulled two pairs of silk boxers from the bag. "I figured only the best should be against our skin tonight."

Michael grabbed the blue boxers from Brian and ran his

hand across the smooth material. The tag sewn into the back was from one of the ritzier designer stores in the downtown area known as the Golden Triangle. The underwear didn't have a price tag. "I thought you were out of Granny's birthday money. These must have been expensive."

"The graduation money came early. Come on, let's see how they look."

The boys quickly stripped out of their clothes. They had changed around one another many times before, so Michael was used to the brief exhibitionism. That's not to say that he didn't sneak a quick glance at Brian's naked body before they pulled up the shorts in unison.

Michael had never worn boxers before. It was an odd sensation to say the least. Ignoring that there was absolutely no support, Michael loved the feel of the silk against his skin. He stepped in front of the mirror to check himself out and wasn't exactly disgusted by what he saw. Brian came up behind him and rubbed his hands up and down Michael's sides.

"Feels nice," Brian said.

"Yeah, but what if I get hard? I'll stick right out."

"I'm sure we can figure out something to do."

Brian sprayed his body with Obsession for Men. Michael enjoyed the smell. He reached for the bottle of Fahrenheit Brian had given him for Christmas and gave his own body a spritz. The two scents mingled together nicely.

"Come on, let's get dressed." Brian went back to the bed for his tux.

Michael laid out his tuxedo beside Brian's. He started dressing with his socks and worked his way up to the pants, belt, and shirt. They had both chosen black vests in place of cummerbunds and picked bow ties with a strap that went around the neck and clipped onto the side. Michael was glad that there was no awkward tying of the ties since he didn't have a clue how to do that. The cuff links did give him a problem at first, but Brian showed him what to do. They slid on their jackets and looked one another over.

"Excellent," Michael said without thinking.

"I know." Brian turned to the mirror. "We look fucking awesome."

"Yes, we do." Michael started toward the door. "Let's show my mom."

Brian grabbed his arm. "Wait a second." He brought Michael back to the mirror and stood beside him. The two boys stared at their reflections.

Michael had never seen Brian look more beautiful.

"Say it, Mikey. I know you want to."

Michael knew what Brian meant, but he was still reluctant to say the words out loud. Then again, he realized that he was with the one person who would not make fun of him. "We look just like Captain Astro and Galaxy Lad when they went to the Lunar Ball in *The Dance of Death*."

Brian smiled. "I'm sure we do. Except for the whole gay part."

"Actually," Michael said, finally ready to share a theory he had been working on, "the more I read of Captain Astro, the more I'm beginning to think he might be gay."

Brian did laugh at this piece of news. "There's no such thing as a gay superhero."

"No, look at this." Michael went for his box of comic books. Each book had its own individual plastic sleeve with a piece of cardboard in it to keep the pages from bending.

Brian pulled him away from the box. "Michael, don't waste your time. A gay superhero wouldn't sell. You're only reading into it things you want to see."

"But—"

"Trust me." Brian gently pulled Michael back to the mirror. "The world isn't ready for it yet. But you were right about one thing. We do look like superheroes."

"You're going to have leftovers for the rest of the week," Rosie said as she finished up the food on her plate.

"No, I'm not," Debbie said. "You're taking half of this home with you."

"So much for the diet."

"Who needs a diet? We get enough exercise running around the diner carrying trays full of food."

"Good point." Rosie reached for a cannoli.

"I wonder what's taking them?" Debbie glanced toward the stairs. *"Beauty and the Beast* is coming on soon."

"Like mother, like son. We've got plenty of time before the show starts. Besides, it's a rerun. You just can't wait to see Michael all dressed up."

"Can I help it if I'm excited about Michael's prom?" Debbie said. "And who gives a damn if the show's a rerun, I could watch it a hundred times. That Vincent is—"

"If you start searching the sewers for a boyfriend, I'm having you locked up."

"Couldn't do any worse in the sewers than I've been doing in the bars."

"We're coming down," Michael yelled.

"Hold on." Debbie took the cannoli out of Rosie's hand and put it down. She then took Rosie by the hand and pulled her into the living room. "Close your eyes."

Rosie gave her a questioning look.

"It's tradition." Debbie waited to confirm that her friend had done as instructed and then closed her own eyes. "Come on down."

She heard footsteps descending the stairs and then the sounds of shifting feet. Michael was probably pushing Brian into place.

"Okay," Michael said.

Debbie opened her eyes. "Holy shit!"

"Thanks, Mom," Michael said with a laugh.

Michael and Brian stood framed between the stairs and

the front door. From the perfectly sculpted hair down to the brightly shining shoes, they looked more like men than she had ever thought before. She assumed that the extra touches like the shined shoes were Brian's doing. The kid had a thing about style.

Debbie felt tears coming to her eyes. "You both look beautiful."

"Handsome," Rosie corrected her. "You both look very handsome."

"They're my boys," Debbie said in a tone of mock anger with tears flowing freely. "If I say they look beautiful, they look fucking beautiful."

"Well, then I guess we're beautiful," Brian said.

"Just one more thing." Debbie went over to the refrigerator. She had to push a few things aside to get what she was looking for. She had hidden them better than she'd thought.

"Enough with the food, Deb," Rosie said, laughing.

Debbie ignored her friend's comment and returned from the kitchen with two plastic boxes. She handed one to Michael and one to Brian. Each box contained a small rose.

"I got these for you," she said, reaching for the tissues and the camera.

"Thanks, Mom," Michael said, honestly touched by the surprise.

Brian looked a little moved as well. "Yeah, thanks, Deb."

"Well, don't just stand there." She held up the camera. "Put them on each other."

Debbie watched through the camera window as the boys pinned their boutonnieres on each other's lapel. Her mind flashed back to her own prom with Michael's father—the real one, not the one that she told him had died in Vietnam. His name was Danny Devore. She hadn't seen him since high school. There were rumors that he was gaining a reputation as a fairly well respected drag queen. He didn't even know he had a son, and Debbie intended to keep it that way. She pushed the memory to the back of her mind and focused on her beautiful child.

Once the roses were firmly in place, the boys stood so Debbie and Rosie could get a good look at the final product.

"Let's get some more pictures," Debbie said.

"Mom—"

"You will pose for as many pictures as I want."

Brian threw his arm around Michael. Through the camera window Debbie could see that her son was happy as he put his arm around his friend. The flash went off. "Hold on, I want another one." She took an additional picture.

"Let me get one with you," Rosie said as she took the camera.

Debbie walked across the room as Brian politely started to move off to the side. "Where the hell do you think you're going?" She grabbed his arm and pulled him back to her. She posed with the boys flanking her.

"Okay, now one with you and Michael," Brian said as he worked his way out of Debbie's grasp.

Debbie let him go and posed with her son. The flash went off again.

"Okay," she said. "Now I want—"

"We've got to go, Mom." Michael started for the door.

"One more thing." She hurried over to the kitchen table. She had to move a couple plates to find what she was looking for, but the envelope was right where she had left it. "This is for you." She came back and handed the envelope to Michael.

He gave her a confused look as he opened the envelope and pulled out the slip of paper. "It's got a number written on it."

"It's a confirmation number. I rented you boys a room at the hotel your prom's at. I don't want Brian driving his car drunk later. This way, I'll know you're safe."

"Mom, we're not—"

"Oh, please, I'm not an idiot. I'm not going to stop you from drinking, but there is no way in hell I'm going to let you drive."

"Thank you, Deb," Brian said.

Debbie could tell that her son wanted to point out that they couldn't afford the room. "Accept the damn gift and shut up," she said before he could open his mouth.

"Thanks, Mom."

"I also took the liberty of pulling an overnight bag together for the two of you." She pointed to Michael's book bag discreetly shoved in a corner. "Just a change of clothes for tomorrow and some toiletries."

"I was wondering what my bag was doing down here," Michael said, picking it up.

Debbie gave both of the boys a peck on the cheek before sending them off on their way. She stayed in the doorway for a moment as she watched them get into Brian's car and drive off.

"A hotel room?" Rosie asked as soon as the door was shut. "If you were worried about them driving, why didn't you just get a limo?"

"The room costs about the same price. And I can't understand paying that much for a car they'll be in for less than an hour round-trip."

"But, Michael and Brian in a hotel room on prom night?"

"There's nothing the boys can do in that hotel room that they couldn't have already done in Michael's room," Debbie said as they went back to the kitchen. "Besides, a limousine is a little too romantic if you ask me. I don't want to go filling Michael's head with any more fantasies about Brian Kinney."

"I don't know that I'd be so understanding if he was my son."

"When Michael first started hanging out with Brian I was glad that he finally had a close friend who he could

share his life with. It didn't take long for me to start worrying that Brian was a bad influence. But after four years of
seeing those boys together, I know I can trust them with
each other. Although I'm beginning to suspect that Brian's
never going to give Michael what he wants."

"And what's that?"

"A night in a hotel room that he could never tell his
mom about."

chapter ten

"We've got enough money to get a couple bottles of stuff," Brian said as he double-parked the Nova in front of the State Store and cut the engine.

"How drunk do you intend to get tonight?" Michael asked.

"You never know when a party might break out. It's best to be prepared."

"Be prepared? I thought you didn't like to be confused with a straight little Boy Scout."

"Good one." Brian smiled. Michael's wit was getting almost as sharp as his.

"Aren't they going to figure out that we're a couple high school students on the way to the prom?"

Michael's constant worrying tended to make Brian laugh. At the same time, Brian liked that someone was doing the worrying for him. "I've been here before. We'll be fine."

The tuxedo-clad boys got out of the car and went into the State Store. Rows of liquor bottles of various shapes and sizes were laid out before them. It was only an hour until closing, but the place was fairly empty. It usually looked like this except around the holiday season.

Brian had heard that in some states one could actually buy liquor at the supermarket. Pennsylvania, however, was not one of those states. The only places that sold the harder alcohol were state-run, closed at nine o'clock at night, and weren't even open on Sundays. It made it all the more difficult for anyone under twenty-one to get good and wasted off anything other than beer.

But Brian Kinney knew he wasn't a beer drinker.

Beer was for men like his father, and he had no intention of being anything like his father.

"Should we get some champagne?" Michael whispered. "To celebrate?"

"Sure," Brian replied in a normal voice. "And you can speak up."

"Sorry."

"It's over there." Brian pointed to the far aisle. "I'm in the mood for something a little harder too."

"When aren't you?" Michael asked as he went in the direction of the champagne.

Brian smiled as he turned down the aisle to his left. His eyes scanned down the shelves past the vodka, rum, and gin until he came upon what he was looking for—his old friend Jack Daniel's. Brian grabbed a bottle and realized he was not alone. Looking down, he saw a small blond-haired boy sitting on the floor holding a teddy bear. The kid appeared to be around six or seven.

"Nice to know I'm not the youngest one here," Brian said to himself before bending down to the boy. "Isn't it a little early to be on the floor?"

"I'm not supposed to talk to strangers," the boy said, looking at his teddy bear.

"Especially strangers in liquor stores, I'm sure. Well, stranger, I'm Brian."

The kid didn't say anything.

Brian looked up and down the aisle. It was empty, but he assumed the kid's parents weren't too far off.

"What's this guy's name?" Brian asked as he tapped the teddy bear on the head.

"Gus."

"Well, hello, Gus. It's nice to meet you." Brian shook the teddy bear's paw, then turned his attention back to the boy. "So now that I know Gus and Gus knows you, I guess that means we're not strangers anymore."

"No, it means you think this bear is real. Which makes you a crazy stranger. That's worse."

Brian had been caught totally off guard by the kid's comment. He was pretty sharp for a six-year-old.

"Justin, don't run off like that." An incredibly Waspy-looking blond woman came hurrying down the aisle. Brian couldn't help but notice that she was carrying a rather expensive bottle of wine.

"I think he's okay," Brian said. "I found him before he moved on to the really hard liquor."

Brian caught the woman off guard much in the same way her son had surprised him. She didn't appear to get the joke at all. "Oh, well, thanks," the woman said, holding out her free hand to her son. The boy took his mother's hand and the pair made their way to the register.

"I got the champagne," Michael said, coming back around the corner holding up a bottle of brut.

"Oh, the four-dollar brand. How quaint." Brian grabbed the bottle and started back toward the champagne aisle. "Are you sure you don't want some Boone's or Mad Dog?" He put the bottle back on the shelf and picked another brand. He didn't really know anything about champagne, so he just picked something from a higher price range. "We got the Jack. We got the sparkling wine. Let's see what other kind of trouble we can get into tonight."

The boys left the State Store after adding bottles of vodka and Southern Comfort to their purchase. They hadn't even been carded, which was quite a statement about how lax the cashier was in his duties.

"These are great fake IDs," Michael said as they got back into the Nova. "I wonder if we're ever going to get to use them."

"That's the thing about confidence, Mikey. Act like you're an adult and the world will accept it for fact."

"Not to mention that people are just too lazy to do their jobs."

"That helps too."

It took twenty minutes to drive from the State Store to the Holiday Inn where the Susquehanna High senior prom was being held. While Michael waited in line to check in, Brian made himself comfortable on a couch and scoped out the action in the lobby. Assorted classmates were passing through on their way to the ballroom in the back. A few guys were coming from the direction of the ballrooms and getting into line to check in. Brian wondered if their girlfriends had any clue that they were renting rooms.

Seeing his paired-up classmates in their finery, Brian wondered what the fuck he was doing going to the prom. It really was such a heterosexually themed event. He knew that he would have fun with his friends, but it just seemed so against type for him. Brian wasn't big on political statements, but somehow it just felt like a lie. And he didn't even know what he would do if elected prom king, but he toyed with a few festive ideas.

Brian saw Michael waving excitedly and remembered the main reason he had decided to come. Michael was kind of excited about the evening. His attitude could sometimes be contagious. And Brian was always up for a good party. He grabbed his bags of alcohol and followed his friend to the room.

*   *   *

"Here we are," Michael said. "Room five oh five."

Michael let Brian in first since he was carrying the bags of alcohol in both hands. Considering Brian's refusal to help with the food the other day at the park, that was all the help Michael was going to provide. He let the door close behind him. The place had a typical Holiday Inn layout with the entrance to the bathroom in the foyer, a dresser, a TV, and a nightstand between the two double beds. Michael had hoped for a single bed to share, but he knew his mom would never have booked it that way.

"This is nice," Michael said, looking over the room. It really wasn't nice at all, but he was trying to keep positive.

"It's a hole." Brian threw himself onto the bed, giving the springs a few test bounces. "But it will certainly do."

"I can't believe our prom is at the Holiday Inn."

"Well, if the prom committee hadn't been so afraid to charge a little extra with the tickets, we could have had it at The William Penn or one of the other hotels downtown." Brian pulled the Jack out of the bag.

Michael threw his backpack on the bed and grabbed a pair of glasses from beside the ice bucket on the dresser. He held them out while Brian poured two heaping drinks.

"Don't you want the champagne?" Michael asked.

"Save it for later. What shall we toast to?"

"Friendship?"

"Simple, yet perfect." Brian held out his glass. "To friendship."

"To friendship." Michael clinked his glass with Brian's.

Michael took a sip of the Jack Daniel's. It burned as it went down his throat. He tried not to make a face as the sour taste hit him full force. Brian had first introduced Michael to the contents of the Kinney liquor cabinet when they were fourteen. Michael still hadn't managed to find a liquor that didn't make him cringe when he drank it.

When Michael turned his attention away from the drink, he caught Brian checking himself out in the mirror over the bureau.

"You know what I think?" Brian asked.

"Usually."

"I don't think we look like Captain Astro and Galaxy Lad."

"Really?"

"I think we look better than that. More like Bruce Wayne and his ward, Dick something."

"Grayson," Michael provided the last name of the character better known as Robin. "And I'd be surprised if you could describe the differences in how Captain Astro looks from Batman when they're not in uniform."

"Batman's rich. That's all the difference I need to know." Brian continued to check out his wares. "Yep, Bruce Wayne."

"You know, the movie is coming out in a couple weeks," Michael said, referring to the Tim Burton film that he was excitedly anticipating. "The AMC is having a midnight showing on the day it opens. Do you want to go?"

"Sounds good to me." Brian took another sip of his drink.

Michael could tell by the look on his friend's face that something was on his mind. "What is it?"

"Thanks for stopping me from coming out to my dad the other day."

"I figured you didn't want to do it like that."

"Not every fag can be lucky enough to have his mom tell him he's gay."

"Yeah." Michael's mom was certainly one in a billion. "Lucky. But I'm sure your parents will handle—"

"I really don't give a fuck what they think." Brian finished off his drink. "I only wanted to tell him because I knew it would piss him off."

"Three weeks," Michael said reassuringly. "All you have to do is make it three more weeks."

"Then orientation, summer session, and soccer camp. Do I know how to plan an escape or what?"

"A little too well."

"I can't wait until I get to the dorm," Brian said. "Did I tell you it's an all-male floor? Imagine the possibilities."

Michael knew that he was supposed to be picturing all-male orgies in the showers, but he couldn't conjure up that particular image. All he could think about was that each guy on the floor provided one more reason for Brian to forget about him.

"We should get back downstairs," Michael said. "They've probably started serving."

"Just one more drink," Brian said lightheartedly. "Before I have to share you with everyone else."

Suddenly, Michael wasn't in such a rush to get down to the prom. Brian poured the Jack and handed a glass to Michael.

"You know, I've been thinking about that whole gay superhero thing you were talking about earlier," Brian said after taking a sip of his drink. "Maybe it's not that far from the truth. I mean, they do wear those tight uniforms."

"That's what I'm saying." Michael drank a little too quickly and felt it rush to his head.

"So that's why you've been hooked on them for so long." Brian took both of their glasses and put them down on the nightstand. "It's just another form of gay erotica."

"Well, they do have some sexual undertones."

Brian got a serious look on his face as he took a step closer to Michael. "So, *Dick*, how about a slide down the batpole?"

"What are you doing?" Michael asked nervously as Brian got closer.

"Want to shoot some of that web fluid? Maybe take a ride on the Astroglider?"

Michael giggled. "Maybe we could take Wonder Woman's invisible jet."

"Maybe you should leave the innuendo to me." Brian sat his friend down on the bed.

"What are you up to?" Michael asked, feeling Brian's hand slide up his thigh.

"Proving that we can be a dynamic duo." Brian leaned in only inches away from Michael's mouth.

Michael closed his eyes, waiting for the kiss to come.

"Will you be my sidekick?" Brian asked.

"Yes."

"Will you follow me wherever I go?"

"Yes."

"Will you do exactly what I say?"

"Yes."

Brian's hands took hold of Michael's dick through his pants. "Are you horny?"

"Hell, yes."

"Good." Brian let go.

Michael's eyes shot open as he felt Brian get off the bed. His body was still tense with anticipation while his mind was full of questions. "What the fuck was that about?"

"I was just getting you in the mood." Brian finished off his drink.

"The mood for what?"

"We're going to get you laid tonight."

Michael stared at his friend. "What do you mean get me laid?"

"It's tradition on prom night for a guy to lose his virginity. I figured it would help if I got you in the mood first. It will help relax you. Tonight you will have sex for the first time."

Oddly enough, Michael was suddenly quite far from being in the mood. "I've had sex before."

"Paying Marsha Grundig five dollars to give you a blow job does not count as having sex."

"Yes, it does."

"Mikey, blow jobs are to sex like the chess club is to cheerleaders."

"Okay, so you got thirteen-fifty on your SATs, stop showing off already," Michael said in a huff.

"I'm sorry. I just thought you might need a little kick start."

Michael wanted to say that the kick start would have been fine so long as Brian got on to ride him afterward, but for some reason chose to remain silent. Besides, there had been far too many puns going around the room earlier anyway. A minute ago, Michael was so ready to have sex. And now, for some reason, it was the furthest thing from his mind.

So much for Brian's plan.

"We should get going," Brian said. "Or we're going to miss the prom."

"Good idea."

chapter eleven

Michael felt a little light-headed when he stood up and wished that he had eaten a bit more of the feast his mom had prepared. He gathered his senses as they rode down in the elevator. Once they were on the ground floor, Michael and Brian made a left turn out of the elevator and followed the signs on the wall through a maze of ballrooms with names like Sunflower, Carnation, and Lily until they reached the Orchid Room.

A trio of juniors sat by a table collecting tickets. The line to get in wasn't long at all. Michael assumed it was because the prom had officially started an hour earlier. Once they showed their tickets, Michael followed Brian into the Orchid Room as Chaka Khan's voice spilled out into the hallway.

I wouldn't lie to you, baby
It's strictly a physical thing

The prom committee had gone overboard with the decorations. Crepe paper and balloons in a variety of bold col-
ors filled every corner of the room, every table, and every
other piece of furniture whether it was nailed down or not.
The centerpieces were truly a work to be admired and
ridiculed. Papier-mâché rainbows with child-size ruby red
shoes on them adorned each tabletop.

"Over the rainbow," Brian said as they entered the
room. "I can't decide if our prom theme is incredibly stupid or inadvertently hysterical."

"I'd say a little of both." Michael looked over the place.
"Kind of like high school."

Once Michael had finally managed to take in the decor,
he noticed that the prom was already in full swing. Dinner
was being served to the students at their tables, while people still littered the dance floor. He saw plenty of classmates that he knew, but none that he was in a rush to
speak to. Michael figured his closest friends were probably
somewhere in the middle of all the dancers.

"What do you say we get our picture taken together to
commemorate the event?" Brian asked.

"Are you serious?"

"Why the hell not?"

Michael liked the idea. Aside from his looking forward
to having a permanent record of his evening with Brian, it

made sense to get the photo out of the way before they got all sweaty from dancing, or—in Brian's case—other activities. Michael was a little uncomfortable about a photo together. Two boys getting their picture taken at the prom was a little more "out" than Michael traditionally liked to be. Then he realized that the photographer was in a little room off to the side of the ballroom. No one would actually see the boys posing together but the guy taking the picture.

That put his mind more at ease.

The line for the prom photo was fairly long. It was full of girls preening in front of their compacts along with boys who acted as if they could not care less about their looks, although Michael caught more than a few of them checking themselves out in the reflective metal trim along the wall. Michael made small talk with the various people around them while Brian—easily one of the most popular kids in school—stayed mostly silent.

Michael, who was popular by association, always felt uncomfortable in these situations, but actually handled it a lot better than Brian did. Michael tended to look for the best in people, while Brian often expected the worst. Both boys had the same friends, but they approached them quite differently. Brian liked to maintain a distance from the kids in line, while Michael preferred the polite banter as they waited.

It took surprisingly little time for the two boys to work their way to the front of the line. Michael attrib-

uted the fast-moving line to a photographer who probably just wanted to get the night over with. They
entered the little room together and were met by a photographer who was easily the most flaming gay man
Michael had ever seen. Considering the circles his mom
traveled in when Uncle Vic was in town, that was saying a lot.

"One at a time, boys," the man said with the intensely
stereotypical lisp heard on those few occasions a gay character was portrayed on TV, usually on *Saturday Night Live*.
Unfortunately, Michael realized this one was for real.
"Where are your dates?"

"We don't have any," Brian replied.

"We were hoping . . . we wanted to have our picture
taken together," Michael replied haltingly.

"Oh." The man drew the word out as long as he could.
He didn't bother to conceal that he was looking the boys
up and down with a leer.

Michael remembered Bill the Troll. This guy was almost
twenty years younger than Bill, but seemed exactly the
same in all the ways that counted.

Brian rolled his eyes and moved to the posing area.
"Can we get this done?"

"Right away," the photographer said. "I don't want to
keep you . . . from anything."

The photographer was clearly making some kind of
innuendo, but Michael ignored it. He just moved next to
Brian and waited for the flash.

His smile brightened when Brian decided to position the two of them in the traditional prom couple pose by sliding Michael in front of him. Brian then reached around Michael and held on to his left hand. Michael knew this was being done to tease the photographer, but he didn't care. For a brief moment he let himself believe that he was actually Brian's date for the night.

The camera flashed.

The moment was over.

"Okay, so just fill out this form and your pictures will be delivered to your homes," the photographer said. "Or you can always stop by the studio to pick the photos up in person."

Michael ignored the man as he wrote his information down on the sheet. He requested double copies of everything, knowing that Brian wouldn't want the photos sent to his house. As soon as Michael wrote the last word on the form, he hurried to get out of the room.

"Kill me if I ever get like that," Michael said once they were free.

"Like you'd have to ask."

While they were getting their picture taken, the music had changed. Now Whitney Houston was singing about wanting to dance with somebody.

"Do you want to go dance?" Brian unintentionally echoed the sentiment of the song.

"Actually, I'd like some food first. I'm a little buzzed."

"I figured." Michael was a bit of a lightweight in comparison to Brian. "Let's grab a table over in the back. Less chance we'll be bothered."

"Okay."

They found a pair of empty seats at a table along the far corner where a lone couple sat. Joshua and Hope were the school's resident outsiders.

Joshua was wearing an old-fashioned dark suit that screamed it was from one of the more eclectic secondhand shops off Liberty Avenue. His girlfriend, Hope, was in a formless black dress with matching black makeup. Michael couldn't be sure, but Joshua seemed to be wearing eyeliner that matched his girlfriend's. They were a pair of loners in every sense of the word and the only couple in the entire school that Michael had no doubt would be happily married someday, unless they both turned out gay.

Either option was equally possible.

It was rare to find people who just didn't care about appearances in a high school full of lemmings that would follow any new trend. Brian actually made small talk with the couple as Michael ate his meal.

The songs continued to change from pop hit to pop hit, until an unexpected song came up. The difference was almost jarring.

Erasure was singing "Oh L'Amour."

Without a word, Joshua and Hope got up and went for the dance floor. Michael assumed it was the only song that would be played tonight that the couple had ever heard.

"The deejay has promise," Brian said.

Michael looked over at the deejay table and wasn't sure if Brian was referring to the guy's musical taste or his potential for a quick fuck after the prom was over. The deejay was young, attractive, and not entirely interested in the high-haired girls gyrating in front of him vying for his attention.

Michael finished chewing a piece of chicken. "Yeah, but you know we'll get the same old crap later, and the evening will end with Donna Summer's 'Last Dance.' I mean, I like disco, but—"

"After the soph hop, junior prom, and various homecoming dances, you get a little sick of that particular song," Brian completed his friend's thought.

"This is the senior prom. You'd think it would end with something special."

"Speaking of getting you laid . . . ," Brian said, never being one to give up on a subject.

"I don't believe that was the topic at hand."

"Yes, but unless all you want tonight is your hand, you should do what I say." Brian wasn't about to drop the subject. "Look at all these hot young guys." He motioned out to the tuxedo-clad classmates around the room. "Every one of them hoping to get some from their date. Three-quarters of them will wind up going home and whacking off. It's our duty to keep the male youth of Susquehanna High School from sexual frustration."

"You've been doing a fairly good job on your own," Michael said with only a slight hint of contempt.

"Yes, but I am only one man." Brian indicated to the room again. "One man among many."

"They do clean up well," Michael said, looking at the sea of tuxedos. The dresses kind of faded into the background for them both. "What is it about a guy in a tux?"

"It's the James Bond thing. All the Bonds look hot in a tux. Well, except Timothy Dalton."

"Look over at Glenn," Michael said. "He looks really good."

"Better than he does naked. I know from experience."

"Glenn's gay?"

"Probably not. But that rarely gets in the way."

"How about Harley?" Michael's eyes were flitting about.

"He shouldn't have worn tails. Hides his cute little ass."

They looked over the room, checking out different guys along the way.

"Hey, isn't Mr. Palmer chaperoning?" Michael asked, carefully broaching the subject. "I bet you'd like to see him in a tux."

"Guess he's not here. I never bothered to ask."

"Disappointed?" Michael asked cautiously.

"I couldn't care less. Stop romanticizing the relationship."

"Sorry."

"But doesn't Todd Weaver look like crap?"

"Whoa," was all Michael could say. His tormentor had

chosen a white tuxedo with a blue vest and tie that matched his date's dress but very little else in this world.

"Suddenly I don't feel so bad about his constant insults," Michael said. "Obviously he's got bigger problems."

"Check out the tux coming this way," Brian said, as close to drooling as he had ever been. "Talk about a body . . . oh my God."

"Andy?" Michael said, mirroring Brian's shock.

Their friend was making the long walk around the dance floor to their table. He looked hotter than either of them had imagined he could look. He finally had his mop of hair cut down to something short and almost sophisticated. The tuxedo he wore draped his body perfectly. The cummerbund he had chosen accentuated his thin waist. He had even forgone his glasses for contacts.

"If I had known he could look this hot, I never would have told you he liked you," Brian said. "Come on, Mikey, now's the time to make your move."

"Knock it off."

"No. It could be your last chance. He's going away next year."

"Not interested."

"Why not?"

"I don't know," Michael replied honestly. "He's just not my type."

"Who gives a damn about type? He looks hot. Fuck him."

"And then what?"

"Graduate. Move on."

"I'm not you," Michael said as Andy approached. The closer he got, the better he looked. Michael wasn't even sure why he was protesting so much.

"I'm aware of that fact," Brian replied. "You spend so much time worrying about sex that you're never going to actually have any sex. Are you waiting to fall in love? 'Cause let me tell you, love seems overrated to me. Do it with a friend. That will probably be more special."

Brian had hit the proverbial nail on the head and yet still didn't get it. "I'm just not interested," Michael said.

"Are you—"

"Drop it," Michael insisted as Andy stepped up to the table.

"Hey, guys," Andy said.

"Andy Stark, don't you look sexy in your formal wear," Brian said with grin.

Andy blushed over the unusual compliment. "Thanks . . . uh . . . you too. Hi, Michael. You . . . you look nice too."

"Thanks," Michael replied, trying to focus on Andy's face instead of checking out his body.

"Here are my favorite guys," Lisa said as she came up to the table and grabbed on to Andy's arm.

Michael was awestruck when he saw Lisa in her dress. She "cleaned up" even better than Andy did. Lisa was wearing a beautiful maroon, off-the-shoulder dress that hung perfectly to accentuate the cleavage that Michael had never noticed before.

If only he weren't gay.

"Wow" was all that would come out of his mouth.

"Ditto," Brian repeated.

"Thank you," she said. "I see you've stolen my date."

"You two are here together?" Michael asked.

"Figures," Brian said, trying not to laugh.

"Come on, let's dance," Lisa said, extending the offer to all the guys.

"Okay," Andy said, but he didn't move. "Michael . . . are you coming?"

"In a second."

Andy and Lisa headed for the dance floor. The music continued to not suck as the Pet Shop Boys sang their remake of Elvis Presley's "Always on My Mind."

Brian couldn't hold in the laughter any longer.

"What's so funny?" Michael asked.

"Your boyfriend and your fag hag going to the prom together." Brian got up from the table.

"He is not my boyfriend. And don't call Lisa a fag hag."

"It's not an insult. At least, I don't think it is. Come on, you have to admit it's cute."

"I don't have to admit anything." Michael stood up.

"I'll admit that looking at Andy in that tux is making me a little stiff."

"Brian!"

"Hey, don't blame me for what happens if you don't take your chance. I'll meet you on the dance floor."

"Where are you going?"

"Over to compliment the deejay on his choice of music," Brian said as he walked away.

Michael watched his friend disappear through the dancers.

He shook his head in resignation as he went to join Lisa and Andy.

You were always on my mind
You were always on my mind.

chapter twelve

Brian spent a few minutes flirting with the deejay and getting a few of his questions answered. Apparently, the deejay—named Dante, believe it or not—wasn't crazy about the prom committee's music selection, which focused a little too much on Bobby Brown and Tone Loc. He managed to mix in a few of his favorites. Brian complimented the guy on his choices and stuck around a few minutes more. He left the conversation open-ended in case he decided to come back later and strike up more than just talk.

Brian went to the dance floor and found his friends gathered in the center. Sharon, Christine, and Ian had joined the group and formed a small circle.

"I didn't expect to see you out here so soon," Michael said as he angled himself away from the group for a moment so they could talk a little more privately.

"The man's working," Brian said into his friend's ear. "You can't just expect him to drop everything for the first cute guy that comes along."

"Most men usually do."

Brian couldn't argue the point. "So, you been making any moves on Andy?"

"Would you please drop it?"

"Consider it dropped." Brian gave his friend a hard look and danced into the center of the group.

Michael looked skeptical.

Brian didn't blame him.

Dante's voice came over the microphone. "The next one is a special request. For Michael."

"What did you do?" Michael asked as the music started up.

Brian just smiled. The familiar sound of horns opened the song he had asked Dante to play.

"Asshole!" Michael yelled over the music.

"What's wrong?" Lisa asked.

The rest of their friends looked concerned.

"Nothing's wrong at all," Brian said as the singing started. "Come on, Mikey, dance."

"I am not going to dance to this song." Michael started to move off the dance floor.

Brian blocked his path. Michael tried to move to the right, but Brian countered the shift using his natural defensive soccer moves.

Goody two, goody two, goody, goody two shoes
Goody two, goody two, goody, goody two shoes

Eventually, Michael gave up and started dancing. Just as Brian knew he would.

The music continued with the likes of Depeche Mode, The Clash, and INXS. Brian was actually beginning to have some fun. He decided to let his guard down for a while and stop scoping out the room for potential fuck buddies.

Michael seemed to be having a good time as well once he got over his anger at the dedication. He appeared oblivious that both Andy and Lisa were trying to position themselves so they were dancing with him. Brian suspected that Michael was aware of what was going on with Andy at least. Michael was the kind of guy who would rather appear clueless than lead someone on. It was a nice trait, but it wouldn't necessarily help in the "getting laid" department. For some reason, Brian's mind flashed to that now classic film *The Last American Virgin*. He shuddered involuntarily.

The lights slowly dimmed and the music returned to more bubblegum favorites with "The Lady in Red."

Christine and Ian locked lips as they pressed their bodies together for the slow song.

Sharon walked right off the dance floor.

"Michael, do you want to dance?" Lisa asked.

"If your date doesn't mind."

Andy looked a little uncomfortable, but acted agreeably. "Sure. Go ahead."

"Come on, Andy." Brian threw his arm around the guy. "Let's go get some punch."

People were shifting around the dance floor as groups morphed into couples while some walked away and others joined in. By the time Brian and Andy got to the punch bowl, there was quite a line.

"Michael and Lisa look cute dancing together," Andy said as he watched them on the dance floor.

"I guess," Brian said. "Too bad she's not his type."

"Really?" Andy said, trying, in vain, not to sound too eager. "What do you think Michael's type is?"

Brian paused for a moment, deciding how he was going to play out this conversation.

It was a quick moment.

"Beats me. I don't think Michael even knows what his type is."

"Oh." Andy sounded slightly disappointed.

"It's a shame too." Brian baited the hook. "Because he doesn't know a good thing when he sees it." He punctuated the statement by noticeably checking out just how good Andy looked in the tux up close.

"This line is taking forever," Andy said uncomfortably. "I could really use a drink."

"You drink?" Brian asked, mildly surprised and thankful for the easy opening.

"Well . . . um . . . no."

"Couldn't be a better time to start. You know, I've got some harder stuff in my room." He loved the double entendre.

"You got a room?"

"Upstairs. Want to see it?"

Andy took a moment to check the line, but Brian knew the guy was just working up his courage. They both looked back to the dance floor, but Michael and Lisa had been swallowed up by the crowd.

"Sure," Andy said. "Why not?"

"Why not, indeed."

Brian led Andy out of the ballroom and back through the maze of halls to the elevator. He stepped inside and pressed the number five.

"Going up," he said with a smile.

Brian remained silent in the elevator and on the walk to the room. He didn't want to scare Andy off. The kid was even more cloistered than Michael was. Hell, he had probably never been kissed before by a guy or a girl. Stellar student, on the school choir, and the model child, he was boring as hell. It's no wonder Brian had never noticed him before.

Brian unlocked the door to Room 505 and ushered Andy inside. He briefly considered putting the Do Not Disturb sign on the handle, but didn't want to push his luck. Things could get more interesting if someone—say Michael—walked in on them.

"Two beds?" Andy asked as he stepped into the room.

"I'm sharing the room with Mikey."

"I should have figured." Andy looked as if he was deciding whether to sit on one of the beds. He chose to stand. "You guys spend a lot of time together."

"That we do." Brian lay on the bed, provocatively stretching to get the glasses and bottle of Jack off the nightstand. "We share everything." He opened the half-empty bottle and poured the drinks. "Here you go."

Andy accepted the drink, but stayed on his feet.

Brian sensed that they were going to get nowhere this way, so he stood as well. "To sharing," he said, clinking his glass against Andy's.

"To sharing," Andy echoed the odd toast.

They both downed their drinks in one shot. Andy's face showed the shock of the quick drink a second later.

"Better slow down there." Brian took Andy's empty glass from his hand and put it with his on the dresser.

"Yeah." Andy steadied himself.

"Is that a real bow tie?" Brian asked, playing with Andy's neckwear.

"It took me a half hour to figure out how to tie it."

"Did it?" Brian pulled at the tie, causing it to unravel. The loose fabric hung down along Andy's chest.

"Brian! It's going to take forever to do that again."

"That's why I went with a clip-on." Brian removed his own tie. "I chose a vest for the same reason. This cummerbund looks like a bit of a challenge to get on and off by yourself." Brian slid his arms into Andy's jacket and around to the back of his body. His fingers worked at the clasp at the back of the cummerbund. It came off with a snap. Brian let it fall to the floor. "Well, that was easier than I thought it would be."

He pressed his body up against Andy's and could feel the hardening in both of their pants.

"Brian, I—"

Brian stopped him from speaking by placing his lips on Andy's mouth.

Andy pulled away, but Brian wouldn't let him go far. "Brian, I don't think—"

"Where did you get this body?" Brian asked as he slid his hands up and down Andy's sides. "And why have you been hiding it?"

"I've been . . . I've been helping my dad at work. He's a contractor."

"I like a man in a tool belt."

"Are you . . . gay?"

Brian replied with another kiss. This time, Andy was a little slower to pull away. Brian released him from his hold. He didn't want to push too hard.

"Does that answer your question?" Brian slid off his jacket.

"I heard rumors." Andy got himself another glass of Jack. The bottle shook as he poured. He lifted the drink to his lips and took a sip. "I never thought—"

"It's all true." Brian took the glass from Andy and finished it off.

"Is Michael—"

"Forget about Michael." Brian put the empty glass back down. "This is about me and you." He slid his hand through Andy's neatly trimmed hair and massaged the back of his neck. "No one has to know."

"Are you sure?"

Brian went in for the kill. Pressing his mouth against Andy's for the third time, he pushed his tongue between Andy's lips. He knew that he had won when he felt Andy's tongue massaging his. They held their kiss for a few moments before Brian broke away.

"Let's see how easily the rest of this comes off," Brian said, sliding Andy's jacket off, then starting to unbutton his shirt. The buttons popped off one by one, and Brian flashed back to the night before his birthday when he had done a vaguely similar thing to Michael. Brian didn't often think of Michael when he was having sex, but every now and then his best friend slipped into his mind.

It was a line he wasn't entirely comfortable crossing.

He refocused back to the situation at hand when Andy gave in and started removing Brian's vest and shirt as well.

Brian and Andy stepped out of their shoes as they admired each other, bare-chested for a moment. Sensing some hesitation, Brian pushed his naked torso against Andy's as their mouths found each other once again. Without breaking their kiss, Brian slid his hands down Andy's back. He increased the pressure of his kiss as he slipped his hands between them and undid Andy's pants, letting them fall to the floor. Andy was wearing a pair of green bikini underwear with a wet spot forming at the top. Brian placed a finger in the waistband.

"Wait," Andy said.

Brian removed his finger from the inside of the cotton bikini, but he didn't stop. He slid his hands around to Andy's back and massaged his ass.

"Is this your first time?" Brian suspected he already knew the answer.

"Well," Andy said, drawing out the word as if debating making some kind of admission.

Brian was intrigued. "Go on."

"Back in camp . . . we used to . . . . we used to have these . . ."

"Circle jerks?"

Andy nodded his head.

"I have something a little different in mind." Brian continued gently rubbing his hands over Andy's underwear as he leaned forward and whispered, "Do you want me to continue?" He slid his hands into the back of the bikinis and grabbed at Andy's flesh.

"Yes."

The underwear was dispatched immediately.

Brian moved his hands to Andy's hard cock and gave it a good, slow stroke. The size caught Brian by surprise. If he had known Andy was packing that kind of meat, he would have made a move much sooner than this.

"Your body just keeps getting more and more impressive."

Andy beamed.

Brian guided Andy to the bed and gave him a gentle push backward. The naked body bounced slightly as Andy leaned back on the pillow.

Brian undid his own pants and dropped them onto the floor along with the red silk boxers. He could tell that his own endowment impressed Andy by the look on his face. Brian stepped forward onto the bed and crawled up to kiss Andy again. He pressed his naked body down and their hard cocks rubbed against each other as they embraced.

Andy finally broke the kiss, breathing heavily.

"Are you ready to take this to the next level?" Brian asked as he lowered his hand and held their cocks together, giving a good squeeze. He was sure Andy had never done this at camp before.

"Yes."

"Tell me what you want."

"What?"

"Tell me what you want."

"I want you."

"What do you want me to do?"

"I want . . . I want you to fuck me."

"What was that?"

"Fuck me."

"Okay."

chapter thirteen

"Have you seen Andy?" Lisa asked as she came back to Michael with the glasses of punch she had insisted on getting them both.

Michael had been trying to ignore that Andy and Brian had disappeared a while ago. Between being an hour late and his unscheduled vanishing act, Brian had missed most of their prom. Then again, Michael assumed that his friend was having much more fun.

He tried to put certain thoughts out of his mind.

"I think he's over there." Michael gave an indirect wave to the side of the room, hoping that Lisa wouldn't go in search of someone who he knew wasn't there.

"They're about to announce king and queen of the prom," she said.

"Andy's not up for king, is he?" Michael tried not to sound too doubtful.

"No, but we were planning to make fun of the winners together. Unless Brian was elected king, of course."

Michael had entirely forgotten that Brian had been nominated. They hadn't really talked about it since the morning of the voting, so it was easy to overlook.

"Where's Brian?"

Michael was afraid that Lisa was going to put two and two together and come up with something. "Probably in the bathroom," he said quickly. "Making sure he looks perfect to accept his crown."

"He does spend a lot of time in front of a mirror for a guy."

"He does, doesn't he?" Michael tried to sound just as confused by the fact as Lisa. He considered calling down to the room to alert his friend to the announcement, but decided not to. It wasn't his responsibility to look after Brian all the time.

Besides, Brian didn't care anyway.

Principal Hogan stepped up to the microphone next to the deejay table. The prom budget was so bare-bones that they didn't even have a stage or a platform for the crowning of king and queen. The "ceremony" was going to be held on the side of the dance floor beside the rest of the commoners.

"Maybe you should get Brian," Lisa suggested to Michael.

"It's his own fault if he misses this." Michael's voice had a bit more edge than he had intended.

Lisa looked as if she had caught on to the anger, but chose not to pursue it.

Principal Hogan gave a fairly long and rambling speech about the school year and his inflated pride with the senior class. The length of the prom speech did not bode well for what their upcoming graduation ceremony had in store for them next week. Once he finally ended his rambling, Hogan pulled out the envelope with the name of the prom king.

"Please don't be Brian. Please don't be Brian," Michael whispered over and over to himself, mumbling softly enough so Lisa couldn't make out what he was saying. It wasn't that he wanted his friend to lose. He just knew that when Brian didn't show up, everyone would be looking at him for an explanation.

"Todd Weaver!" Hogan announced.

"Word!" Todd shouted. It sounded stupid coming from someone so incredibly white.

Lackluster cheers went up throughout the room. Todd's "boys," Jason and Steven, pumped their arms in the air, letting out Arsenio Hall's trademark whooping.

They sounded like idiots too.

"Figures," Lisa said with disgust. "Like that asshole deserves it. I can't believe he got a majority of the vote."

"You know what Mrs. Linden says, 'The masses are asses,'" Michael said, quoting their English teacher.

"Ain't it the truth."

Principal Hogan pulled a second envelope out of his jacket. "And the prom queen is—"

"Michael Novotny!" Todd yelled into the microphone.

Principal Hogan glared at Todd while only a smattering of people laughed. Michael took that to mean that he wasn't the only one in the room getting tired of Todd's lame insults. At least, that's what he wanted to believe.

"What an ass. Why the hell does he keep acting like you're gay?" Lisa looked at Michael for a response.

Michael had a look not unlike that of a queer trapped in the headlights. It was one thing for him to remain silent on the issue of his sexuality, but it was quite another for him to flat out lie to one of his closest friends about it. He could have just covered up the whole thing by making a cut about Todd, or a simple "I don't know," but Michael was tired of the entire topic.

The length of his pause was enough of an answer.

"Oh." Lisa's face registered a mix of shock, disappointment, and sadness.

Neither of them even noticed that Missy Caldwell's name was announced as prom queen.

"Lisa, it's just—"

"No," she said, backing away from him. "You don't have to explain." She took off through the crowd in the direction of the rest rooms as "Somewhere over the Rainbow" began to play.

In that moment, Michael realized that both his mom and Brian had been right about the way Lisa felt toward him. Suddenly, he felt very, very stupid.

Michael tried to discreetly follow Lisa, hoping not to attract attention. He saw her hurry past Brian as he came back into the ballroom. Michael froze, not wanting to see his best friend at that moment. A minute later Andy came into the room. He wasn't wearing his tie and the top button of his shirt was undone.

"What's with Lisa?" Brian asked as he came up to Michael.

"She figured out my little secret."

"I assume she didn't take the news well."

"Imagine how she'd feel if she knew you just fucked her prom date," Michael said, not bothering to lower his voice.

"On the bright side, she would probably have felt worse if *you* fucked her prom date. See, it's already not as bad as you thought."

Michael didn't know what to say.

"You had your chance," Brian said.

"Hey, guys, what's up?" Andy asked as he joined them.

Michael left without saying a word. Once he was out of the ballroom, he made his way over to the women's rest room. He wanted to go in to check on Lisa, but he knew that he couldn't.

While he was waiting, Jen Yang came out the door.

"Jen, did you see Lisa in there?" Michael asked.

"Yeah, she came running in a minute ago."

"She wasn't"—Michael didn't want to ask—"crying?"

"Not that I noticed," Jen said, putting his mind at ease. "She was too busy throwing up."

Michael's heart ached. This was the most horrific reaction he could ever have imagined to telling someone he was gay. Not that he had actually told her.

"Are you guys drinking?" Jen asked excitedly. "Do you have anything?"

"We drank it all," Michael said, covering up the truth with Jen's convenient story.

"Damn." Jen headed back for the ballroom.

Michael took a seat by the rest room. He watched as various girls went in and out as a cloud of hairspray was released each time the door opened. He considered getting either Sharon or Christine to check on Lisa, but didn't want to bring more people in on the fiasco. After what seemed an eternity, she finally came out into the hall.

"Lisa," Michael said as he shot out of his seat. She had been crying. "Are you okay? I didn't want to tell you like that."

"What are you talking about?"

"About me being"—Michael struggled to actually say the word aloud—"gay."

"Oh, that." Lisa laughed it off. "Do you think I didn't know?"

"But you ran straight for the bathroom."

"I think the chicken was bad. I'm better now. Let's go back."

"Okay." Michael didn't believe her for a second.

They ran into Andy as soon as they stepped into the ballroom.

"Lisa, I've been looking all over for you," he said, refusing to look in Michael's direction.

He had probably figured out that Michael knew his secret. It was surprising the number of truths coming out at the prom. Andy was obviously uncomfortable with Michael knowing and was trying to avoid him. And that was just fine with Michael. He didn't really feel like looking at Andy right now, or Brian either.

"Let's dance," Lisa said, nearly dragging Andy to the dance floor.

Michael saw Brian on the dance floor with Sharon. He didn't feel like dancing, so he sat down at a table with some of the other members of the newspaper staff. He spent the next hour talking about absolutely nothing.

"Having fun?" Brian asked as he finally made his way over to Michael's table toward the end of the evening.

"Loads," Michael said with an edge as he got up from the table. He didn't expect Brian to be discreet and he wanted to get as much room away from his friends as possible for whatever Brian was going to say. Michael wasn't ready to come out to the rest of the senior class on prom night.

"Going anywhere in particular?" Brian asked.

Michael realized that he had walked himself into a corner.

"I invited a bunch of people back to our room for an after-prom party," Brian said.

"It's nice you're being so generous with the room my mom rented."

"Christine and Ian have some wine in their limo," Brian said, ignoring Michael's remark. "And I thought we could pop the champagne."

"Are you sure you didn't want to use the room for sex with anyone else first?"

"No, I think I'm fine for the night," Brian answered honestly.

The deejay's voice came over the microphone. "Ladies and gentlemen, it's time for the last dance."

"I've never been so happy to hear Donna Summer before," Michael said.

"Oh, I made a special request," Brian said. "I think you'll like this song better than the last one I had Dante play for you."

An unfamiliar tune came over the sound system. Michael didn't recognize the song, but he could feel its pulsing beat in his body.

Brian held out his hand. "Dance with me, Mikey."

The song was slow and romantic, the kind one danced to with a lover. In Michael's opinion it was not the kind of song boys danced to together at the senior prom.

Boy/girl couples were filling the dance floor for the final song of the evening.

"Are you insane?" Michael asked, believing the answer to be yes. "I am not going to dance to this with you."

"Come on. Show them all that you don't care. After next week, you'll probably never see any of these people ever again. Dance with your best friend."

"Brian, I realize you don't give a damn what people think. But I do. And I'm not ready for this."

"Fine. I'll dance by myself. But someday, I promise . . . you and I will dance to this song."

So darlin' save the last dance for me

Michael watched as Brian made his way to the dance floor without looking back. He positioned himself by the couples whom he knew best and started swaying to the music alone. At first, people looked at him strangely since it was so unusual to see someone moving by himself to a slow song in the middle of the dance floor.

As the third verse started, Sharon split from the guy she was dancing with and joined Brian in his solitary dance. The constantly linked Christine and Ian soon followed suit, as did Andy and Lisa. Then, one by one, the other couples around Brian broke off until half the dance floor was filled with lone dancers slowly swaying to the music.

It was the power Brian had over people. He could make them do whatever he wanted.

It was a power Michael often found himself fighting against.

It was a power Michael knew he would never possess.

chapter fourteen

Michael should have known that he couldn't escape Donna Summer entirely.

"Macarthur Park" was booming through the speakers as he took his now familiar spot leaning against the bar at Babylon.

It was the club's first official "Disco Night."

He watched Brian alone on the dance floor and tried not to make the obvious connection with the way the prom had ended. The situation was entirely different, anyway. Brian was gyrating beneath one of the dancing boys. He seemed to be rather intently focused on the guy. Michael was even a little surprised when he saw Brian put some money in the go-go boy's G-string. He wished he could hear what they were saying.

Michael turned his attention to his drink when the crowd obscured his view of Brian.

It had been almost twenty-four hours since the prom had ended. Michael had stayed up all night partying with his friends in his hotel room. He didn't have as much fun as he should have since he barely said a word to Brian or Andy throughout the night. Similarly, Lisa had hardly spoken to him as well.

He knew he couldn't do anything about that until she was ready.

As for the other issue, even with all the hot, sweaty men of Babylon laid out before him, all he could think about was Brian and Andy naked in the hotel room Michael's mother had rented. He knew that he was being a bit unreasonable since he had repeatedly denied any interest in Andy.

But that wasn't the reason he had been jealous in the first place.

His unwarranted anger toward Brian did not stop him from coming to Babylon with him. But it did prevent him from allowing himself to have too much fun. Which was exactly the reason why Brian was out on the dance floor and Michael was at the bar.

On the bright side, he did have a chance to finish the rum and Coke this time.

He motioned to the bartender to pour him another.

"Back again," a familiar gruff voice said beside him.

"Not again," Michael said, hoping that the troll would

take the hint. He ignored the man while he paid for his drink.

"Is your friend in the back room again?" Bill asked.

Michael finally looked over at his stalker and saw that Bill had really taken the Disco Night theme to heart. The polyester shirt was open down to his belly button, exposing a massively hairy chest and almost as much gold jewelry as Mr. T wore—although Michael was sure Bill's was fake. He could only stomach a quick glimpse down at the white pants that looked to be about three sizes too small.

"My friend went to the bathroom," Michael lied. "He'll be right back." He hoped that what he said was true. For all he knew, Brian *could* be in the back room again.

"Would you like me to keep you company?"

"That's okay."

"You know, it's good that you came back here so soon," Bill said, undaunted. "Never know when these clubs are going to disappear. Gay clubs like this don't have much of a shelf life in Pittsburgh. I give this place a year."

Michael thought the guy was insane. The place was even more crowded than it had been on opening night, if that was even possible.

"Here comes my friend," Michael said with relief as he saw Brian coming toward him. He threw his arm around Brian the second he was within reach.

"Nice to see your mood's changed," Brian said.

Michael ignored him for the moment and said to Bill, "Well, he's here. Thanks for keeping me company."

"Are you—"

"I'm fine now," Michael insisted. "You can go."

Bill skulked off without saying another word.

"What was that about?" Brian asked.

"Never mind," Michael replied coldly. He removed his arm from Brian's shoulder.

"Are you ever planning to get over the fact that I fucked around with Andy?"

Michael chose not to respond. He took a sip from his fresh rum and Coke.

"I've arranged a little peace offering," Brian teased, pointing to the dance floor.

In the time that Brian had been out of view, he had moved from the go-go boys to the club's general populace.

A pair of men in their early twenties were dancing seductively and giving Michael the once-over. Michael couldn't help but think that Brian knew how to pick them.

"The blond's yours," Brian said.

Michael had never been given a guy before.

He checked out the blond. The guy was wearing a thin, white T-shirt so tight that even at a distance Michael could see the guy's erect nipples trying to poke through the material. The equally tight pants also revealed something else that seemed to be erect and quite impressive.

"It's just like you to think that a quickie makes a good apology," Michael said.

"I don't think I have anything to apologize for. I just thought this might be a good way to move on."

"I am not about to fool around in the disgusting back room of this club."

Brian smiled.

Michael hated the smile. It was the one that Brian always had on his face when he knew he had won.

"I had something else in mind," Brian said.

Fifteen minutes later, the Nova was idling in park down by the Monongahela River. Rain was pouring on the roof outside, forcing them to keep the windows closed. Steam had already built up on the glass and nothing was even happening inside the car.

Yet.

Some inane song was on the AM radio, but the volume was so low that it could hardly be heard. Brian was in the front seat with the brunet, while Michael shared the large backseat with the blond.

The guy had said his name was John . . . or Don . . . or maybe even Ron. The music had been so loud at Babylon that it was difficult to hear. They had shared a quick dance to "I Will Survive" before Brian had led their foursome out to the street.

The conversation in the car had been limited to lies Brian had told about their being students at Carnegie Mellon. Michael wondered if he was ever going to go to Babylon and not lie about being a student at a college he didn't attend.

John/Ron/Don slid across the large backseat and put his arm around Michael without a trace of subtlety.

Michael was uncomfortable with the move, but he didn't fight it. For some reason, Brian's having sex with Andy had lowered Michael's resolve considerably. The romantic in him had gone home early this night and left in his place a guy who just wanted to get off. He wasn't about to have full-on sex with the blond, but there were plenty of other things they could do together.

Naturally, Michael certainly wasn't expecting to be romanced in the backseat of Brian's car, but he was caught slightly off guard when Don/John/Ron's face moved closer to his without warning. He was about to venture into largely unexplored territory. Michael turned his head and felt a pair of lips caress his neck. He wasn't so much playing hard to get as he was trying to work up his willpower to enjoy the encounter. The blond's maneuvers were certainly helping.

Michael looked to the front seat and saw Brian smoking a joint. He hadn't seen where the pot had come from, but assumed that it belonged to his friend as opposed to the brunet, whose name Michael had caught. It was Charlie.

Michael only remembered that because his own middle name was Charles.

One of the few rules that Brian adhered to in life was never to smoke other people's pot. He only trusted drugs that he got from friends and shared with friends. As Brian passed the joint to Charlie, Michael relaxed a bit. He waited for it to make the rounds while Ron/Don/John planted light kisses on his neck. Maybe this wouldn't be so bad.

Charlie stretched his arm into the backseat and tapped his friend on the shoulder. "Ron, here you go."

"Ron!" Michael said, cementing the name in his head.

"What?" Ron asked as he took the joint from Charlie.

"Nothing," Michael said, covering for the little slipup. "I liked what you were doing." That part was true.

Ron inhaled the pot smoke and held it in his lungs for a moment. After he released the smoke, he said, "Good, because I'd like to do some more." He handed the joint to Michael and returned to the task at hand.

Michael took a deep breath and sucked on the joint. He was using the drug's powers to strengthen his resolve. Brian's carefree attitude toward sex was often a turnoff for Michael, but he never really understood why. If Brian was to be believed, sex was only a game to be played like any other diversion. It didn't need to be all hearts and flowers. It didn't need to be everlasting love. It didn't need to be any other cliché found on the easy-listening station.

Michael made his decision.

He was going to have fun tonight.

If it killed him.

From his position behind the passenger seat, Michael could see that Brian and Charlie were already making out. As Michael expelled the smoke from his lungs, he slid his right hand under Ron's chin and pulled the guy's face up toward his own mouth. He braced himself for the kiss.

For the first time since they'd parked, Michael could hear the song on the radio. Some guy was singing about a woman who was whining about *no huggy no kissy until I get a wedding ring*.

"Can you turn that off?" Michael asked in utter annoyance. All he needed was Meat Loaf's "Paradise by the Dashboard Light" to come on next to make the evening even more trite.

Brian shut the radio off. "Better?"

At that moment, Ron's hand had slid down to Michael's pants.

"Oh, yeah," Michael said as both answer and reaction.

Ron looked up at him, leaning forward.

Michael closed his eyes as Ron's lips pressed against his own. Their mouths met and their tongues tangled with intensity. Michael didn't feel the same passion he had felt during Brian's birthday kiss—or even, surprisingly, what he had felt with Andy during spin the bottle— but he was certainly feeling something more than just the heat of the joint between his fingers. When Ron finally pulled back from the kiss, Michael offered the joint to his new friend.

Ron sucked on the weed while it was still in Michael's hand.

"Thanks," Ron said.

Michael saw Brian leaning back against the door. Somehow he was already shirtless. Charlie was nowhere to be seen, but Michael could imagine what was going on. From his vantage point all he could do was imagine. The back of the seat blocked his view of all the interesting stuff, which was a bit disappointing. He had often seen Brian naked, but had never done so while Brian's dick was active.

Brian smiled at his friend and held out a hand.

Michael passed the joint back to its owner and focused on the cute guy unbuttoning his shirt. Ron pushed aside the material and left a trail of soft kisses down Michael's bare chest. Michael placed his hands on either side of Ron's head and pulled it back up to his mouth for another deep kiss. He did this more for courage than for romance. But he did enjoy the kissing too.

Ron's hands continued exploring below the belt, rubbing over the denim. Michael's dick was hardening from the manipulations. He glided his own hands down to Ron's ass, rubbing it in a circular motion. The tension was palpable in their kiss as Ron's hands worked at undoing Michael's pants. The button came undone and the zipper was pulled down. Ron broke their kiss. The look on his face silently requested permission to proceed.

Michael lifted his hips in response.

His pants were down to his knees in moments. For the first time in his life, Michael was hard and mostly naked with another man. Actually, three other men, but that was only a technicality. Ron's hand grabbed Michael's dick. The grip was strong, but his fingers moved gently across the skin.

Michael let out a moan of pleasure.

Ron repeated his trail of kisses down Michael's body. This time, there were no pants to get in the way. His mouth was soon around Michael's dick.

The pleasure was intense. Michael had only had one hurried blow job prior to this backseat encounter. It didn't even compare to the magic that Ron's tongue was performing. The suction of his vacuum kiss nearly pulled Michael off the seat.

Ron gave fucking good head.

Michael's nearly unrestrained moans of appreciation spurred Ron on to work even harder.

Once Michael's eyes were able to focus, he saw that Brian was staring at him with a look of surprise, success, and, of course, delight. Michael panicked for a moment. It would be unfair if Brian could see him in action, when Michael couldn't see Brian. But Michael quickly realized that Ron's head was blocking any potential peep show. Besides, Brian wasn't looking down, he was looking right into Michael's eyes.

Brian took a hit from his joint and offered it to Michael.

Michael accepted the joint and inhaled its fragrant aroma, then passed it back.

Ron's head moved more furiously. Michael knew he couldn't hold on much longer. He could feel the cum churning in his balls.

"Wait," Brian whispered to him as if he knew how close Michael was.

Ron's tongue was doing spectacular things as it tickled Michael's dick.

"Wait," Brian whispered again with his own face reflecting the pleasure he was experiencing.

Michael could feel himself growing more sensitive. He was on the brink. It took all his energy to focus on holding back.

"Wait," Brian insisted.

Michael's toes curled in his shoes and he clenched the muscles in his stomach.

"Now," Brian said.

Michael let himself go as he shot a load of cum into Ron's mouth. The nerves throughout his body exploded along with his dick as the orgasm washed over him. His body relaxed and his face took on an expression of pure joy that he suspected mirrored the look that Brian was giving him.

They never stopped staring into each other's eyes.

chapter fifteen

Michael was still reliving the pleasure of Saturday night in his mind Monday morning during his walk to school. The best part of the evening, in his opinion, was that Ron hadn't requested any reciprocation. Not that Michael hadn't been willing to return the favor, but he wasn't entirely sure that he was ready to do so under Brian's watchful eye. He'd rather have some practice before performing in front of an audience. Michael had wanted to get the guy's number, but Brian had driven them away once he'd dropped Ron and Charlie back at the club.

And just like that, Michael had gotten over his anger at Brian. It certainly helped that Brian had arranged for Michael's first real man-on-man experience—ignoring the allusions to pimping in that statement, of course. Not only that, but Michael knew that he wouldn't have gone through with it if Brian hadn't been there spurring him on. Brian tended to make Michael act more boldly. He wished he could feel that way all the time.

There was no academic reason to come to school Monday morning since the homeroom teachers had even stopped taking attendance. In fact, Brian had not seen fit to do so, which explained why Michael was once again walking. But this was the day yearbooks were being handed out and the final issue of the school paper was released. Besides, there was something cool about coming to school for the first time after what he considered as losing his virginity—or at least part of it. He felt this urge to brag about it, but there really wasn't anyone there he could brag to. The one person he could tell already knew.

Michael had expected Brian to come pick him up, but after waiting a half hour and getting no answer when he called the Kinney home, Michael went to school on his own. He wondered what his friend could be up to, but with Mr. Brian Kinney it could be anything.

They had separated Saturday night and hadn't been in contact since. Michael casually speculated whether a murder had been committed in the Kinney household. It would explain why no one had answered the phone when he called.

He shuddered when he thought that not entirely unlikely.

He rarely spent twenty-four hours out of contact with

Brian. At the very least they usually spoke on the phone once a day. This did not bode well for the future. He worried how often these gaps in communication would occur once they were both in college. He would find out soon enough since Brian was moving into his dorm in exactly two weeks.

Michael didn't bother waiting for Lisa at their prearranged meeting place. He was running late and figured she was already at school. Michael went straight for the auditorium once he got there. He was hoping to find Brian, but doubted that would happen.

The first person he ran into, oddly enough, was Lisa.

"Hi," he said, not knowing what else to add.

"Hi."

Awkward silence.

"Did you have fun at Hersheypark?" Michael tried small talk. He knew that Lisa's family had made the long drive out to the park over the weekend to celebrate her little brother's birthday. With everything she'd done since Friday, he figured she was exhausted.

"It was okay," she said. "Not as much fun as when we went after the junior prom."

That last word seemed to echo through the auditorium.

"Yeah. Look, about the other night—"

"I'm sorry," she immediately replied. "I know it wasn't the reaction you were hoping for."

"You threw up."

More awkward silence.

"Have you ever wanted something really bad?"

He didn't have to think long to answer. "Yes."

"And did you ever have that moment when you realized you were never going to get what you wanted?"

It was weird for Michael to think that she was talking about him. It was even stranger for him to be equating their conversation to his feelings for his best friend. He was beginning to suspect that he might never have anything more than friendship with Brian.

But that didn't stop him from hoping.

"That's what it was like," Lisa said. "I can't tell you how many years I spent . . . pining for you. Then I finally realized I'd never have you." She smiled. "And the chicken really was pretty raunchy."

Michael laughed to cut the tension *and* because he remembered how the chicken had tasted. "I never meant to lead you on. If I had known, I would have said something. I would have told you the truth."

"I know. I'm not mad at you. Just disappointed that things are never going to be the way I wanted them to be."

"You're my closest friend in the world, besides Brian. I'm always going to be here for you. You know that."

"You'd better be." Her smile wasn't entirely forced. "Because I've been getting this weird vibe from Andy lately. I think he may like me and I'm going to need you to do some investigating."

"Uh-huh," Michael said, trying to figure out a way to

extricate them both from this one. "I'll see what I can find out. Don't do anything until I get back to you."

"Will do."

"So we're okay?"

"We're okay." She reached into her book bag and pulled out a folder. "And this is for you."

Michael took the folder from Lisa and opened it to find several copies of the *Susquehanna Spotlight*.

"It's the second issue off the press," she said. "And the third, fourth, and fifth. I know your mom would want them. I kept the first for myself."

"Naturally." He opened the paper to his article.

The Time of My Life—Growing Up in the Eighties
By Michael C. Novotny

After three years of working on the paper, Michael still got a rush when he saw his name in print. He was impressed by the look of the article as well as the professional appearance of the paper overall. Since it was the senior class's farewell issue, Lisa had gone all out to make it special. It was more than just a recording of the baseball team's scores and a review of the school show. The issue was full of special tributes and columns that really gave the writers a chance to shine.

"So where's Brian?" Lisa asked.

Michael shrugged his shoulders.

"It would be a shame if he didn't get his yearbook."

"Wouldn't it?" Michael replied sarcastically.

"Problem?"

"No, just the usual frustrations."

"You two guys aren't . . ."

"Fighting? No, not really. At least, not anymore. I just expected him to pick me up this morning and he never bothered to call."

"Oh. But actually, what I was wondering was . . . if you guys were—"

"Oh, God, no," he said quickly.

"Good. I don't think I'm ready to handle that."

If she only knew.

"I better get onstage," she said. "It looks like Mrs. Linden is about to start."

"Need help?"

"I've got it covered. But wait for me before you head over to the yearbook signing party."

"Will do."

Michael watched Lisa as she walked up to the stage to hand out the newspapers beside Mrs. Linden, who was giving out the yearbooks. He considered Lisa's body for a moment as it got farther from him. If he ever was to be with a woman, he realized that he could do a lot worse than Lisa. It was only because of whatever strange spin of the wheel that he didn't want her the way she wanted him. Of course, the wheel took an even stranger spin when he thought about her expressing an interest in Andy. It was as if that damned clichéd wheel kept landing on "Bankrupt" or "Lose a Turn."

Or maybe there was something in the school water supply.

"Michael," a familiar voice said from behind him.

He didn't want to turn around, but he had no choice. "Andy, how are you?"

It was beginning to feel like "closure day" at Susquehanna High School. Convenient that it would be happening right before graduation.

"Good," Andy replied. They were both still a bit uncomfortable around one another.

Michael wondered if Andy still had that crush on him or if all the feelings had gone away with one sweaty encounter with Brian. At this point, Michael wasn't sure if he was more jealous of Andy or Brian and wondered if he might still have a chance with the guy in front of him. Now that he had fooled around with a stranger, the concept of having some fun with a friend didn't seem so unappealing. If his backseat encounter with Ron had taught him anything, it was that indiscriminate sex could be more enjoyable than he had previously believed. And, yes, Michael still counted blow jobs as sex.

"Is Brian around?" Andy asked, dashing any hopes Michael had of the crush continuing.

"Haven't seen him." Michael shifted his attention to the stage. Mrs. Linden was beginning to give out yearbooks to the line of students that had formed along the wall.

"But he is coming in today?"

"I said, I haven't seen him." Michael was growing

annoyed for no real reason. "He doesn't run his schedule by me."

"I was just thinking that since you guys are friends . . ." Andy said.

Michael caught the unmistakable tone in Andy's voice. It was hope. Suddenly the anger and jealousy subsided. Andy was Michael's friend too. They had known each other since seventh grade. Andy needed to know the truth.

"Andy, don't do this."

"Don't do what?" he asked, honestly confused.

Lisa's words rang in his ears. "Pining for Brian."

Andy's face went red. "I'm not . . . I don't—"

"I know what happened," Michael said, choosing his words carefully. "Don't worry, I'm not going to say anything. But you have to know . . . Brian was just having fun. It's what he does. It didn't really mean anything."

"I know that," Andy said only somewhat convincingly.

"I figured you did." Michael went along with the lie. "I just wanted to make sure you weren't—"

"Thanks, I appreciate it."

"Listen. If you ever—"

"I should go help Lisa give out the papers," Andy said as he started for the stage.

"Of course you should," Michael said, mostly to himself.

Another missed opportunity.

He watched as Andy walked away from him and wondered what if? Then he tensed up a bit when he saw Lisa awkwardly hug Andy when he walked up to her. This was not good.

Michael got in line for his yearbook along with the rest of the senior class. It didn't take long for him to get up to the stage. Mrs. Linden had a fairly smooth operation going, and by the time Michael made it onstage she had run out of books in at least three boxes. When she peeled back the lid from a new box, two dozen fake coiled snakes jumped out at her, scaring the teacher and just about everyone in the immediate area.

After a brief moment, the laughter started.

"Can't you people wait until graduation?" Mrs. Linden yelled.

Then, seemingly from out of nowhere, Principal Hogan came hurrying down the aisle and onto the stage. "No, they will not wait until graduation," he bellowed, more toward the students than Mrs. Linden. "Let me be perfectly clear about this. There will be no pranks during commencement this year. Anyone caught trying to disrupt the ceremony will have to come in the next day with their parents to pick up their diploma. Am I making myself clear?"

Assorted mumbles filled the room.

"Good," he said as he stepped back down from the stage. "Carry on."

"He says that every year," a student behind Michael said.

Michael knew that to be true. The graduation ceremony Wednesday night would continue the tradition. It would be a prank-fest of the highest magnitude. It was the main reason the students were looking forward to the otherwise boring ceremony.

No one knew when the tradition had started, but each graduating class took great pride in trying to come up with more original gags than the one before. The goal was always the same: to bring the ceremony to a halt for any length of time or, at the very least, make it more interesting.

"Michael, that was a lovely article you wrote for the paper," Mrs. Linden said as she handed him his yearbook. "Lisa slipped me an advance copy."

"Thanks."

"It really captured the spirit of youth today."

"I hoped it would." He wasn't just kissing up to the teacher; he had actually meant it. Sure, he hadn't exactly thought of his article in the exact terms that she had used, but that was the overall effect he had been going for.

"So, what are your plans for college?"

Michael was acutely aware that the people behind him wanted their yearbooks. That was just like Mrs. Linden. She was organized enough to keep the line moving until she felt like chatting it up with a student for a few minutes. Michael knew that he wasn't going to move until she decided the conversation was over.

"I'm going to Allegheny in the fall," he replied.

"Oh. That's a nice school."

Michael couldn't help but suspect that she was trying to mask her disappointment. He didn't know whether to be pleased that she thought he deserved better or upset that she thought less of his school choice—not that it was a choice.

"Brian hasn't picked up his yearbook yet. Is he here?"

"Why does everyone keep asking me where Brian is?" Michael asked, beginning to get annoyed again.

"Because you two are always together," Mrs. Linden replied simply. She was unaware of how upsetting the repetitive question was becoming. "Why don't you take his yearbook too? Save him the wait."

"Sure." Michael took the extra yearbook. Assuming their chat was over, he started across the stage, waving to Lisa and Andy as he went back down the steps and took a seat in the front row.

Since he had promised to wait for Lisa, he opened up his yearbook and flipped through the pages. Like every other student in the room, he was looking for himself and counting the number of times he appeared. He was also counting every one of Brian's photos and comparing the two numbers.

In addition to his posed graduation photo, Michael's picture appeared seven other times in the yearbook—in various candid shots as well as his group photos with the newspaper staff and student council. He thought that was a nice enough number considering how many students were in the class.

Brian appeared no less than sixteen times. Between Homecoming Court, the soccer team photos, and general

shots around the school, his presence was quite notice-
able.

Funny how he seemed to be the only senior who didn't
care enough to actually come in and pick up the book himself.

By the time Michael was through examining the yearbook, the line had worked itself down fairly well. Lisa and
Andy were finishing up with the newspapers, so he joined
them to get the last few out of the way. Once that was
done, the three of them went over to the lunchroom,
where the yearbook signing party was held.

It looked as if the prom committee had been through
the room with all the leftover decorations from Friday
night. The usually cold and unimposing room was
awash in crepe paper and balloons. The decorations
were pointless, since everyone's head was buried in a
yearbook.

The trio grabbed a table with their other friends who
were already dutifully scribbling in each other's yearbook.
Michael joined in the exchange and—like the good little
friend he knew himself to be—made sure that everyone
signed Brian's yearbook as well.

He started with his circle of friends and then moved on
to the general populace. After an hour of that, Michael had
had enough of the false sentiments he was receiving. There
were only so many times he wanted to read "It's been
real!" in his yearbook. He didn't really care to collect notes
from everyone in the room. Michael closed his book,

grabbed Brian's from some kid he didn't even know, and said good-bye to his friends.

He would see them all at graduation rehearsal tomorrow anyway.

Once Michael was outside the school, he pointed himself in the direction of Brian's house. His curiosity as to what had kept his friend from school overwhelmed any passing feelings of resentment he had for the lack of contact over the past day. Dozens of different scenarios ran through his mind in the twenty minutes it took him to walk to the Kinney home.

He rang the bell and waited. The Nova was parked in front of the house, so he knew Brian was home at least. It took a few minutes before Brian answered the door in his underwear.

"Who are you fucking this early in the day?"

"Regretfully, no one." Brian rubbed the sleep from his eyes. "I overslept."

"Which explains the morning wood in your shorts," Michael said, surprising even himself with his boldness. "I was hoping it was something more interesting."

"That was last night. You should have seen him."

"Wait a minute," Michael said as he pulled Brian's yearbook out of his book bag. "You mean you had sex with a different guy every night this weekend?"

Brian smiled the Kinney smile.

"I don't want to know." Michael handed Brian his yearbook. "I picked this up for you."

"And you got it signed for me too," Brian said in a forced appreciative tone. "That was nice. Where did you sign?"

"I didn't yet. I wanted to think about what I was going to say first."

Brian flipped through the pages. "Don't I look nice?" Then he started laughing. "I almost forgot about this."

"What's so funny?"

Brian held up the page to Michael. It was the section with photos devoted to the students elected Most Likely to Succeed and other such nonsense. Actually, it wasn't really nonsense since Andy had been picked to be most success-ful. Brian appeared on the page twice. First he showed up—logically enough—as Class Flirt. But it was his second appearance that he had found so humorous.

Most Athletic.

"Who else were they going to choose?" Michael asked.

"Sad, isn't it? A school whose Most Athletic student doesn't give a shit about sports."

"For not giving a shit, you did pretty well for yourself." Michael read off Brian's list of accomplishments: "'All-State Soccer Team, Student Athlete of the Year, Scholarship to Carnegie Mellon University.'"

"Yeah, whatever good *that* did me. Do you know how many schools I applied to and the only one that wanted me was Carnegie Mellon."

"You got into a bunch of schools."

"Yeah, but they were the only one offering me a full scholarship."

Michael hadn't realized how close he had come to Brian's moving much farther away than just across town. He pushed that thought aside since he couldn't believe that he was hearing Brian complain about his choice of school, considering where Michael was going next year. "It's not like you played a sport where schools were fighting to get players."

"True. I never really liked how bruised I could get in football, and I have no interest in baseball beside the nice tight uniforms."

"And it *is* Carnegie Mellon."

"Exactly. I couldn't even get out of the city limits. Don't they play soccer in New York or California? Hell, I'd even settle for Utah just to get the hell out of here. . . . Well, maybe not Utah."

Michael tried to ignore how intent Brian was in getting as far from Pittsburgh as he could. "Wait a minute, wasn't the sports banquet Saturday night?"

"I think so," Brian said. "Why?"

"Weren't you were supposed to pick up the Student Athlete of the Year award?"

"Sounds vaguely familiar."

"You went to Babylon instead of picking up one of the most prestigious awards our school gives out?"

"I had much more fun at Babylon than I would have at the banquet. I can always pick up the award this summer. It would give me one last chance to visit with Gary."

"Always good to have a backup plan."

"Words to live by," Brian agreed. "Give me your year-book."

"You don't have to sign it right now," Michael said as they exchanged books. "You can take some time to think of what you want to say."

"I will."

chapter sixteen

"Get in here!" Debbie yelled as she opened the door before her brother could even ring the bell.

"What do you have, radar?" Vic asked as his sister wrapped him up in a big hug before he could even put down his suitcase.

"No. Gaydar!" She held on tightly and refused to let go.

"Deb, I can't breathe." He pretended to gasp for breath.

She finally released him. "What the hell took you so long?"

"The train was running two hours late." He put down his suitcase. "It's not like I had any control over the situation. Where's Michael?"

"He's upstairs getting ready. Can you believe it? My boy is graduating high school!"

"I hope so, or I just took one hell of a train ride for nothing."

"Knock it off, smart-ass." She gave him another hug. When she released him, her tone plummeted to serious. "I thought you should know, I haven't told Michael about . . . you yet."

"Still?" Vic was surprised by the news. "Deb, you've got to tell him before . . . anything happens."

"I know," she said in an uncharacteristically soft voice.

Debbie and Michael talked about safe sex often. They talked about repercussions. They talked about disease. But when faced with the possibility of death so close to home, Debbie couldn't bring herself to talk to her son about it. Every time she tried, she just saw herself burying him in the ground. The way she knew she would one day have to do with her brother.

"Do you want me to—"

"No," she said, a little too quickly. "I'll tell him. It's just . . . there's been so much going on lately with the prom and graduation. I . . . I didn't want this hanging over him. It's supposed to be a happy time for him."

Vic thought over what she was saying. "I understand. I won't say anything."

"I promise, I'll tell him before you leave. Once he accepts the news, then we can talk to him together."

"Well, that gives you two weeks."

"The guest room is all cleaned and ready for you. And I've got our outfits ready for the What a Drag Ball."

"And who are we going to be this year?" he asked.

"Cho-Cho San and Pinkerton."

"*Madame Butterfly*," he said, sounding impressed. "Since when have you been into opera?"

"What opera?" she asked, feigning ignorance. "I'm talking about the movie."

Vic laughed. "You'll make a wonderful Cary Grant."

"And you'll be a lovely geisha. You're sticking around for the PFLAG picnic, right?"

"Wouldn't miss it. You've got a better itinerary planned for me than that lousy gay cruise I went on."

"True, but I don't give out free margaritas on leather night."

Michael heard his mom open the front door. He cursed silently under his breath because he had wanted to be ready when his uncle arrived, but he had just gotten out of the shower and still had to throw on his clothes. He finished drying off as he decided what to wear.

He could have gone a couple different routes. Even though the ceremony was being held outside in the evening, it could get warm on the football field. It would be fine for him to wear shorts since he would have his graduation gown covering him up. But he suspected that Brian would be getting dressed up for the ceremony. His friend tended to look his best at any event. That helped Michael decide as he reached into the closet for his best pair of pants and a nice button oxford.

It took him only a couple minutes to dress. He considered going with a tie, but decided against it. Since he didn't really like to get all dressed up, there was only so far he would go. After one last check of himself in the mirror, he hurried downstairs.

"Uncle Vic!" he exclaimed as he jumped off the bottom step and gave his favorite relative a hug. He hadn't seen Vic since Christmas and was thrilled that he could make the trip down for graduation.

"Hello, Michael. How's the graduate?"

"Doing great." Michael grabbed his uncle's bag and put it by the stairs so it would be out of the way. "How was the train ride?"

"Long." Vic handed Michael a gift. It was thin and rectangular, obviously a book. "Here you go."

Michael looked at his mom. "Should I open it now or wait until later?"

"Have I ever made you wait to open a gift before in your life?"

Michael was already ripping open the paper. It was a book. *"All I Really Need to Know I Learned in Kindergarten,"* he read off the title. "Great, so you're telling me I just wasted twelve years of my life?"

"Better to find out now than twenty years from now," Vic said.

Michael opened the cover and found what his thank-you card would later refer to as "a very generous gift." He gave his uncle another hug. "Thanks."

"It's the least I could do."

"Come on, there's food in the kitchen," Debbie said.

"Of course there is." Vic gave his nephew a wink. "When isn't there—" Vic stopped when he reached the table. "Deb, I have never seen so much food in my life."

"The Kinneys might be coming," she said.

"*Might* be coming?" The kitchen table and counters were covered with food. "And how many people are they bringing if they do?"

"There's more in the fridge," Michael said. He and his uncle shot each other a look. They usually shared warm-natured laughs at Debbie's expense when they were together. "You should have seen what she made last week for the prom. And there were only four of us that night."

"My Michael is only graduating high school once," Debbie said, playing along as if she were offended. "I'm going to celebrate. Now shut up, you little pricks."

Both Michael and Vic broke down in laughter.

Debbie had a huge smile on her face. "Both my boys are here." She pulled her son and her brother together into a hug.

"Mom, what are you wearing?" Michael asked in horror as his face was pressed up against her chest.

"You like it?" Debbie released her family and posed for them. She had on a black skirt with a white blouse and blue blazer. "I just got it at Wanamaker's."

It was the most distinguished outfit Michael had ever seen her in.

But Michael wasn't asking about the outfit. "I meant the pin."

"Oh, this." Debbie pointed to a round, pink metal pin on her lapel. "It says 'Proud PFLAG Mom.' I got it in a little store on Liberty called Encounters. They have a ton of pins with funny little quotes. T-shirts too."

"You can't wear that," Michael said.

"Of course I can. I'm a proud PFLAG mom."

"Not at my graduation you're not. Take it off."

"Michael Novotny, you may be graduating today, but I am still your mother. You do not speak to me in that tone."

"I'm sorry. But could you please take the pin off? I don't need you announcing that I'm gay to the whole school."

"It's just a pin. I didn't rent a billboard."

"Deb," Vic interjected. "Maybe you shouldn't wear it."

"Fine." She took off the pin. "I just wanted people to know that I'm proud of my gay son, even if he's not proud of himself."

Michael was torn between anger at her comment and appreciation that she was such an understanding parent. "Mom," he said delicately, "how about tonight I'm not your gay son, I'm just your son?"

"Well, aren't you the wise little shit." She gave him a hug. She held him for a moment before letting go.

"I learned from the best," he replied.

"Damn right you did." She looked over her table.

"Should we wait for the Kinneys to eat?" Vic asked.

"Do that and we could starve," Deb said as she handed her brother a plate.

"Jack, why aren't you ready yet?" Mrs. Kinney's voice carried all the way up to Brian's room.

"The ceremony doesn't start for two hours," Mr. Kinney said. "We've got plenty of time."

Brian continued to fix his hair while checking himself out in the mirror and trying to ignore his parents' voices.

"We have to go to that insufferable Novotny woman's house," Brian's mom said without even trying to conceal her voice. "Now get upstairs and change."

Brian could hear his father getting out of the recliner. He shut his bedroom door for fear that the man would feel the need to stop in on his way to his bedroom.

Mrs. Kinney was normally a quiet, unimposing woman, especially around her husband. But she always managed to come out of her shell and take charge for a public event. It was important to her that outside the house the Kinneys look at all times the picture-perfect nuclear family.

Inside the house was an entirely different matter.

There was a knock at Brian's bedroom door.

Brian ignored it while he straightened his tie. Most guys would be complaining about having to dress nicely only to be covered up by a graduation gown. Brian was different. He liked to dress up almost as much as he liked to undress.

The knock came again. "Brian, it's me," his sister said. "Open up."

He took one more glance at himself at the mirror before getting the door.

"Very nice," Claire said, impressed, as she came into the room.

"Thanks."

"I just wanted to make sure you were almost ready since dad's getting dressed." She sat on his bed. It wouldn't take Jack Kinney long to pull himself together, and he would want to leave the moment that he was done.

"I heard." Brian considered throwing on his dress jacket. He decided against it since it could get warm underneath the graduation gown. "I'm taking my own car."

"Looking forward to college?" Claire was never good at small talk, yet that never stopped her from trying. "You're moving in—what? Two weeks?"

"Twelve days." If she gave him a moment, he could probably rattle off the hours, minutes, and seconds. "I get the feeling you're leading somewhere again. Are we going to have these little talks before every significant event in my life?"

"Why are you so hard to talk to?"

"Why are you always trying to talk to me? You don't really need to play the big sister all the time. Telling me what to do. Making sure I'm okay."

"Someone's got to look out for you."

"Is that what you think you're doing? Looking out for me?" Brian wasn't sure how getting on his case about things from time to time constituted looking out for him.

Then again, it wasn't as if Claire had any role models in the house to show her the proper way. "I think I do well enough on my own."

"Well, I'm here if you need me."

Brian considered opening up to his sister for a moment. It would be nice to be honest to someone in the house for a change.

"Brian! Claire!" Mr. Kinney yelled from downstairs. "We're leaving!"

The moment passed.

"Time to go," Claire said, immediately leaving the room.

His dad must have gotten ready in record time. Nice to know the man didn't feel the need to take the milestone seriously enough to spend some extra making sure he looked good.

Brian followed his sister into the hall. He had intended to sign Michael's yearbook first, so he could bring it with him, but he didn't want to keep his dad waiting. Brian prepared himself to be on his best behavior so his father wouldn't find any reason to ruin the night.

"Well, don't you look pretty all gussied up," Jack Kinney said when he saw his son.

Brian bit his tongue—literally—and focused on the pain. It was easier than dealing with the pain in front of him.

"Thank you," he said.

"Brian is taking his own car." Mrs. Kinney spouted out instructions like a drill sergeant so there was no diverting from her plan. "We'll follow him over to the Novotnys' home. We're only going to stay long enough for a drink and maybe a quick bite and then head over to the school."

No one bothered to respond.

Brian's parents and his sister went out the back door to the garage while he made his way to the front door to get his car. Leaving the house quickly and quietly was something they all had a lot of practice doing. It was no wonder Brian had such an easy time with school fire drills.

As he heard the back door close, Brian took one last moment to look at himself in the mirror they had in what amounted to a foyer. He wasn't usually such a mirror queen, but this was a significant moment. He was about to leave his childhood behind. Sure, one could say that he had done that in the school locker room at age fourteen, but this was different. As much as Brian tried to act as if graduation were an inconsequential ceremony, it did signify the end of an important time in his life and the beginning of a new one.

He straightened his tie one last time and took a moment to imagine the possibilities.

chapter seventeen

Michael stared at his feet as he leaned against the kitchen wall. He had never heard the house so quiet before. It was like the silence in the moment right before the planet Krypton blew up in *Superman: The Movie*. Michael wished that the ground would open up and swallow him the way it had the Kryptonians.

Mr. and Mrs. Kinney were sitting on the couch with Claire. They were picking at the food on their paper plates. Uncle Vic and Michael's mom were sitting on chairs they had brought in from the kitchen. Brian was leaning on the wall beside Michael. No one was saying a word.

"It's a shame you lost your camera," Debbie said, finally breaking the silence, speaking in Mrs. Kinney's general direction. "But don't worry, I'll be happy to make copies of all the photos."

"Thank you." Mrs. Kinney politely nodded.

The first thing they had done when the Kinneys arrived was to take the ritual photos. Michael and Brian had donned their black caps and gowns for the family-and-friend-shots. Mrs. Kinney actually seemed caught off guard by the photo op and acted as if she had spent the afternoon looking for the camera and could not find it.

No one in the room bought the story. Obviously, she had simply forgotten.

The boys tried to take the gowns off when they were done, but Debbie insisted they keep them on and drive over to the ceremony that way. Michael was probably the only one in the room who knew the reason for the request. This way everyone in the neighborhood would know that Michael Novotny was graduating today.

"So, Victor," Mrs. Kinney broke the silence. "Do you have a lady friend in New York?"

"Mom," Brian pleaded, but Michael knew it was hopeless.

"Uh, no," Vic replied. "No lady friend."

"I hear those New York women can be pretty sophisticated," Mr. Kinney chimed in. "Probably just society snobs."

"Something like that." Vic changed the subject. "So, boys, how was the prom?"

Michael quickly responded, "It was—"

"Yeah, I wanted to talk about that," Jack said. "Vic, what do you think about those boys going together instead of getting dates? Would you have gone with a guy to your prom?"

Michael knew that his uncle was smart enough not to come out to the Kinneys. It would just lead places no one wanted to go on graduation night.

Debbie saved her brother from answering. "I think it's wonderful that two friends could be so comfortable with one another. Who gives a damn if it isn't the norm? Don't you think so, Joan?"

Brian's mom looked at her husband before answering. "Debbie, you do tend to lean toward the more . . . eccentric side of things."

On the surface the answer was perfectly noncommittal, but underneath it was clearly meant as an insult. Michael braced for his mom's response.

"Yeah, I guess I do," Debbie said. "But who wants to lead a common life?"

"I just think a mother has a responsibility to set a good example for her children," Mrs. Kinney replied.

"Well, it's just Mikey and me, so I don't really need to put on an act in front of him."

"Pity."

Debbie clearly wanted to respond, but she stopped herself. Michael saw Vic reach over and take his sister's hand, presumably to give her support. They wouldn't do anything to ruin his night. The Kinneys, on the other hand, wouldn't be so inclined as to worry about Brian that way. They sat on the couch as if Brian's mom hadn't just insulted Michael's mom. Although Claire looked a little guilty, even though she hadn't said anything since she'd walked in the door.

"Michael and I better get going," Brian said, moving from his space on the wall. "They want us to show up an hour before the ceremony begins."

The room was a flurry of sudden activity as everyone stood.

"We should go too," Debbie agreed. "Be sure to get good seats."

"Good idea," Mrs. Kinney agreed rather quickly.

"I'll ride with Brian," Michael said.

Seconds later there was a mass exodus from the Novotny home. A wave of relief could be felt as all went to their respective cars.

"Well, that was fun," Michael said with sarcasm as the Nova took off down the road.

Billy Joel was singing on the radio.

This is the time to remember
'Cause it will not last forever

Michael did not care for the song's message at all.

The AM station played the song repeatedly at this time of year in conjunction with the various graduation ceremonies in the area. It started around the time Pitt held its commencement in early May and continued through the last week in June. Michael liked Billy Joel, but was getting entirely sick of this song.

It took them only a few minutes to drive from Michael's house to the school. They were early enough to get a good spot in the parking lot for the football field.

With four hundred students in the graduating class, the ceremony was too large to fit into the auditorium and accommodate everyone's family. So, every year graduation was held in the William Pitt Memorial Football Stadium. The venue was actually quite impressive. Instead of a few metal risers around the field, it was an actual stadium with concrete stands, a broadcast booth, and even an electric scoreboard.

Schools from all over the area played their games at Susquehanna High.

Brian pulled his car into a spot near the exit so it would be easier to get out once the ceremony was over. He actually took up two spots so that the car didn't get dinged. Michael felt uncomfortable from the glare they received from other people pulling into the lot, but Brian didn't seem to care.

Michael got out of the car quickly. "Do you need to get anything out of the trunk?"

"Why would I?" Brian started walking across the parking lot.

"Oh, I don't know. Maybe something for pulling a prank or two?"

"And why would you think I'd be doing that?" Brian asked innocently.

"You mean the kid that glued Mrs. Renfrew's butt to the toilet seat in the teachers' lounge doesn't have anything planned for graduation?" Michael said skeptically. "I don't buy it."

"Michael, we are about to become high school graduates. Pranks are for children."

"So is spin the bottle. Didn't stop you the other day."

Brian flashed "the smile" as they went around to the lot behind the visitors' seating.

A number of students were already there in caps and gowns. Some of them had messages written on their caps in masking-tape letters that could easily be removed when everything was returned after the ceremony:

Class of '89

I Passed!

Will Work 4 Food

Michael didn't even come close to having Brian's fashion sense, and even he found the caps incredibly tacky.

"I hope this doesn't run too long," Brian said. "I'd much rather get straight to the partying."

"If yesterday's rehearsal is any indication, we could be here until midnight." Michael was exaggerating of course, but the rehearsal had run far longer than anyone had imagined. It was even worse because all Michael could think of during the prolonged event was that he needed to get to Buzzy's Comics to see what was new in the Tuesday comic book delivery.

"What's Jake doing here?" Michael asked when he saw Brian's personal mechanic lurking at the side of the field. "I thought he got left back."

"Excuse me for a minute." Brian started off toward Jake.

Michael grabbed his friend's arm. "You *are* up to something, aren't you?"

"Not at all," Brian said innocently as he removed Michael's hand from his arm.

Michael watched as Brian went off. He stood uncomfortably alone for a few minutes while Brian just talked to Jake. Oddly enough, they didn't look as if they were going to go off for a quickie.

"Hey, Michael," Andy said from behind him.

Michael turned. "Hey."

"Where's—"

"Don't say it."

Andy laughed. "Sorry. Lisa sent me over to get you guys. She has her camera and wants to get some pictures."

Michael looked over to the side and saw that Lisa had staked out an area under a tree away from the gathering mass of students. As they had learned the other day during the graduation rehearsal, the lot they were standing in was going to fill up fast.

"Brian's over with Jake Thompson," Michael said, answering the question he wouldn't let Andy ask. At least the two of them seemed much more comfortable with each other than they had been earlier in the week. "He shouldn't be long."

"What's Jake doing here?" Michael couldn't help but notice a slight twinge of jealousy in Andy's voice.

"Beats me. Brian's probably setting up a deal so that Jake will continue to work on the Nova next year since he'll still be here and have access to the shop."

"Things always have a way of working out for Brian, don't they?"

"You have no idea."

Michael waved to the side of the field and caught Brian's eye, then motioned over to where Lisa was standing. When Brian nodded, Michael and Andy started walking to their camera-ready friend.

"Hey, Michael." Lisa gave him a hug. Things seemed to be better with her as well. "Excited?"

"I guess," Michael said. "Looking forward to Missy's party later?"

"Promises to be the social event of the season."

"Before you ask," Andy interrupted, "Brian will be over in a minute."

"Well, then let me get a picture of the two of you," Lisa said.

Both Michael and Andy paused for a moment. "Sure," they said in unintentional unison. Lisa held up her camera and the boys awkwardly tried to pose themselves. They finally settled on putting an uncomfortable arm around each other.

"Smile," Lisa said as she took the picture.

"Aww, isn't that cute," Brian said as he came up behind Lisa.

"Get in the picture," Lisa ordered, using the same tone she usually took when someone was late turning in an article to the paper.

"Yes, ma'am." Brian gave her a mock salute, then stepped up to the other boys. "I get to be in the middle." He pushed his way between the pair.

"You wish," Michael mumbled just loud enough for Andy to hear.

Andy laughed. He didn't seem as shy around Michael as he used to be.

Several more variations of poses were attempted. As more and more graduates arrived, Lisa called Sharon, Christine, Ian, and some other friends over to the impromptu photo session. The atmosphere was relaxed and informal until Principal Hogan walked up carrying an electronic megaphone.

"Attention, graduates," he said into the mouthpiece. A screech came out the device, blasting the eardrums of everyone behind the stands. The principal made an adjustment at the base and continued, "I need everyone to line up in their places. Homeroom advisers, please make sure everyone is in alphabetical order." When the principal took the megaphone from his mouth, a black ring circled his lips.

The students—and more than a few teachers—burst out laughing.

"Let the fun begin," Brian said mischievously.

"I hate it that we have to sit in order," Lisa said. "Like I want to experience one of my life's biggest milestones sitting beside Todd Weaver."

"I wouldn't trade seats with you for all the money in the world," Andy said.

Michael thought the exact same thing.

Of course, Andy did have one of the best seats in the house. As class valedictorian, he got to sit onstage, but he was going to have to give a speech in front of over a thousand people. There were drawbacks.

Sharon had it a bit worse though. She had to *sing* in front of the packed stadium.

Everyone wished Andy and Sharon luck before going their separate directions.

Lisa held back for a second with Michael. She was watching Andy walk to the head of the line.

"So what do you think?" she asked, indicating with her eyes. "Did you find out anything for me?"

"About you and Andy?" Michael made it look as if he were seriously thinking it over. "I think you can do better."

"Than class valedictorian?"

"Why start something up before you go off to Penn?" he asked, not wanting to out Andy. "Keep yourself open.

Never know who you could meet in college." In a school that large he couldn't help but think of all the gay men she could develop a crush on freshman year alone.

Suddenly he was jealous of her.

She seemed to think about what he had said for a moment.

"Can you believe this?" she asked after obviously making up her mind to move on. "Back when we were playing house in the third grade, I never thought that someday we'd really be graduating."

"I know. Is it just me or did it all happen a lot faster than you expected?"

"Yeah." She gave him a kiss on the cheek. "A lot faster. Well, we better get moving."

"Say hi to Todd Weaver for me."

She gave him a swipe on the arm.

Michael and Lisa split up as they joined the four hundred students moving through the lot, attempting to find the assigned spaces they had received during the rehearsal. It was quite a production since the area they were in could barely hold half that number. A considerable amount of pushing and jostling for position had to be done. Michael got banged around several times.

The last hit knocked off his cap.

It was back on his head before he could even bend to pick it up.

"There you go, Mikey," Todd Weaver said.

Michael's entire body tensed. "Shouldn't you be over with the *W*'s?"

"I'm getting there, dude. I just realized that this is probably the last time we'll see each other . . . before college that is."

"Well, have a nice summer," Michael said, moving off.

Todd grabbed hold of Michael's arm. "Look, I just wanted to apologize for all the razzing I did. It was all just good fun." He held out his hand.

Michael stared at the hand a moment, examining it. From what he could see, it didn't look to have a joy buzzer, egg, or any other booby trap. He took the hand and gave it a weak shake.

"That's a boy," Todd said. "No hard feelings."

"No."

Todd smiled and walked away.

Michael didn't believe for a moment that Todd was being genuine in his apology, but he didn't really care. This was the last he would have to see of the creep for the rest of the summer. And then the odds were slim that they would have any classes together at Allegheny in the fall.

As Michael took his place with the other *N*'s he could hear snickering around him. He self-consciously checked his back to make sure that Todd hadn't stuck a Kick Me sign or something on it. Once he was sure nothing was there, he started looking around for some other gag, but didn't see anything. He put the laughter out of his mind when the orchestra started to play the graduation march.

Principal Hogan led the graduates out of the lot.

"Pomp and Circumstance" played over and over and over as the four hundred students made their way onto the field. When the *K*'s started moving, Michael looked for Brian in line ahead of him, but he couldn't see his friend. And he was sure that he had seen Jessica King and Henry Kirkland go out together. When the *N*'s finally started walking, he felt a tap on his shoulder.

"Ready to start our lives?" Brian asked.

"What are you doing here?" Michael whispered. "We're supposed to be in alphabetical order."

"We're outside. Why are you whispering? And who gives a damn about alphabetical order? They're not giving us our diplomas until after the ceremony."

The music got louder as the *N*'s moved past the visitors' stands. When Michael stepped onto the field, he realized that it was too late for Brian to get back in his place. Besides, since it didn't matter, Michael would prefer to spend the ceremony sitting with Brian.

For the second time in the past few minutes, Michael felt his cap come off his head. This time, Brian had taken it off him.

"What are you doing?"

Brian held the cap out to Michael by way of explanation.

A word was written on the top of the cap in masking-tape letters:

FAG

Michael could hear Todd Weaver's familiar laughter over the orchestra. He refused to look back as he continued walking out onto the field. He did hear Lisa curse and what sounded like a smack and assumed his friend was at the back of the line defending him.

His first thought was that he hoped his mother hadn't seen it. It was one thing to be embarrassed in front of friends, it was quite another to be embarrassed in front of his mom. But then he realized that she was the one person whom he wouldn't have to worry about being embarrassed around.

"Don't let that asshole get to you." Brian started to peel the tape off the cap.

"No," Michael said, taking back the cap and placing it on his head. The words were still branded across the top. "I have no intention of letting him win."

He continued on to his seat with head held high.

"Well done, Mikey," Brian said.

The ceremony opened with Sharon signing the national anthem, followed by a beautiful—though humorous—rendition of "Wind Beneath My Wings." Most people didn't notice that she made a few strategic changes to certain words in the song that altered the meaning of the piece. The students who laughed because they got the joke also received a few strange looks from those who did not.

Michael tensed when Andy got up to give his speech. Not only was he nervous for his friend for having to speak in front of everyone, but standing up at the podium like that made Andy a tempting target for pranksters. Luckily, nothing bad happened. In fact, Michael found himself even a little moved by Andy's words, especially the part he included about the tragedy in Tiananmen.

The prank-fest did continue with several moonings, a streaker, and a firecracker going off that accidentally caught Todd's gown on fire during Principal Hogan's never-ending speech. Michael thought that, overall, the gags were a bit of a letdown. But then he realized that whatever Brian was up to hadn't happened yet.

"These pranks suck," Michael said, hoping to pry something out of his friend.

The graduates were all going up to the stage to accept the blank pieces of paper that were standing in for their diplomas. With four hundred students, this part of the ceremony would take the longest—besides Principal Hogan's speech.

"The firecracker was a nice touch," Brian said noncommittally.

"Only because it set a piece of Todd's graduation gown on fire."

"You know what they say about children and matches."

Their exchange seemed to end, but Michael still didn't have an answer to his question.

"So?" he prodded.

"So what?"

"What are you planning?"

"You were the one who told me Hogan was going to punish anyone who played a prank." Brian smiled. "I'm planning on picking up my diploma tonight."

Michael didn't buy it for a second. "I can't believe you won't tell your best friend."

There was a long pause. Michael could tell that Brian was mentally debating.

"You'll see soon enough."

Michael leaned back into his metal chair. The ceremony was almost over. If he knew Brian—which he did—the last prank would be the best.

After another minute, the line had reached the *N*'s. The row stood as one and made their way up to the stage. Michael immediately remembered that the word FAG was emblazoned on his graduation cap. He panicked, wishing that he had taken it off earlier. It was one thing to walk out en masse and fade into the crowd, but now his name was about to be announced over the microphone as he stood on the stage. He considered just taking off the cap and quickly ripping off the words, but at this point it would be totally obvious.

Besides, it would be letting Todd Weaver win.

He felt a pair of hands on his shoulders, giving a little squeeze. Brian seemed aware of the anxiety and was providing much needed support. He was lending Michael the strength he needed to step onto the stage and accept his diploma. As Brian let go, Michael turned and brushed his hand against his friend's lip. The cuts had long since healed, but the bond remained.

Michael walked up the steps and handed the slip of paper with his name on it to the teacher standing by the microphone. He walked across the stage tall and proud.

"Michael Novotny," the teacher said as he accepted his fake diploma from the principal.

He could hear his mom and uncle screaming from their seats and gave a nod in their direction.

As he stepped off the platform, he heard the teacher read, "Brian . . . uh . . . Brian Kinney."

Michael looked back and saw the principal with an expression on his face that could only be described as annoyance. Well, no, it could also be described as pissed off beyond belief. Hogan took the alphabetical order seriously and was visibly upset that *Kinney* was in the middle of the *N*'s.

Michael waited at the bottom of the steps for Brian to join him. The two walked back to their seats arm in arm. The rest of the students collected their fake diplomas in due course, and the line continued to move along uneventfully until Todd Weaver took the stage.

"I wonder what he's going to do now," Michael said.

"Probably something—" Brian didn't get to finish what he was saying.

Todd Weaver suddenly disappeared.

"What the—"

Todd's head popped up through the stage floor. He

looked a little dazed. Someone had rigged a trapdoor and Todd had fallen through.

The laughter started with those students nearest to the stage and moved quickly like a wave over the rest of the graduating class. Michael also swore that he heard laughter coming from the parents in the audience. He suspected that his mom was laughing loudest among them.

Apparently, everyone was a little tired of Todd Weaver.

"Mikey," Brian said, still laughing, "I didn't know you had it in you."

"What do you mean? I didn't do this. You did."

"No, I didn't. I wouldn't waste my final high school prank on Todd Weaver."

Michael could tell that his friend was being honest.

"Well, if you didn't do it and I didn't do it . . ." Michael thought it over. Whoever had set the trap needed to be near the stage—or on it—to pull off the prank. The person also had to have access to the kinds of tools needed to do what was done. He or she also needed a reason to target Todd Weaver.

Michael remembered that Andy's father was a contractor and had an impressive array of tools in his garage. Since the stage had been sitting out overnight, it wouldn't have been difficult for Andy to sneak onto the field and set it up. Then Michael realized that *he* was the reason Todd had been set up. Maybe Andy did still have a bit of that crush.

Michael could not help but be pleased to think Andy's feelings had survived even after a night with Brian. He looked up at the row of students seated onstage and saw Andy looking back at him with anticipation.

"Oh my God," Michael said. "It was Andy."

"No shit?" Brian looked up to the stage.

They both gave Andy the thumbs-up.

Michael didn't think that he had ever seen Andy look so happy before. He felt a bit of regret that he hadn't made his move with Andy when he had had the chance. Michael suspected that if he tried anything now, Andy would still be receptive to his advances. However, Michael found something unpleasant in picking up Brian's discards.

Once Todd Weaver was fished out of the hole in the floor, the ceremony continued with the rest of the students carefully navigating their way across the stage. Once the last student took her seat, Michael remembered that Brian's prank was yet to come.

The class president took the stage. He gave a relatively brief speech that ended, "I hereby accept these diplomas on behalf of the Susquehanna High School graduating class of 1989."

Once the last word was out of his mouth, the class threw their graduation caps into the air. Michael watched as the FAG cap briefly mingled with all the others.

As the caps all came raining down, music blared through the stadium sound system.

This was not part of the program.

It's astounding
Time is fleeting

But that couldn't be the prank. It was too simple.

All eyes looked to the broadcast booth at the top of the stands. Michael suddenly figured out what Jake was doing at the ceremony. He was on the audiovisual squad and had probably volunteered to work the sound system.

The vice principal was already banging on the door to the booth. Michael knew that the only other entrance would require the vice principal to work his way through the stands and run all the way around back. It would give Jake a good three minutes before he had to worry about getting out of the booth.

The students around Michael began to point. At first he thought they were pointing at the booth itself, but he quickly realized that everyone was looking above it.

Two guys were standing on the top of the booth.

They were dancing to the music.

They were wearing nothing but G-strings.

Michael couldn't see their faces clearly, but he didn't have to. He knew exactly who they were since he had seen them dancing at Babylon on both of the nights he had been there. They were the same guys that he had seen Brian with during their last visit.

Michael gave a sideways glance.

Brian was smiling his smile.

The entire senior class yelled, "Let's do the time warp again!"

And then four hundred graduates, two go-go boys, and a surprising number of people in the stands took a jump to the left.

chapter eighteen

Brian pushed his way through the crowd with Michael on his heels. He was pleasantly surprised that his friend had kept the taped insult on his cap through the entire ceremony. It was the kind of statement Michael needed to make for himself. Brian was even more pleased when Michael had had the forethought to grab someone else's cap when the graduates all threw theirs up into the air. The statement would have meant something entirely different when they reunited with their parents.

He was dying to know who got stuck with the FAG cap.

"Do you think they got out all right?" Michael asked as they wove through their classmates' families. "They really weren't up there for too long. Although I'm sure Jake is probably in some trouble right now."

Brian still felt the buzz off his graduation prank. It had

the perfect amount of audacity and subtlety. Though it was difficult to think of two nearly naked men as being subtle. Brian didn't believe in crass, overblown statements. A little song and dance was just what their graduation required.

"Any good schemer has his contingency plans in place," Brian said. "I'm sure the dancers got off okay. Or, they will this weekend when I thank them."

"What about Jake?"

"Every good plan can suffer casualties." Brian continued to scan the crowd. He didn't really feel the need to stop off and say hi to his parents, but knew it was expected. Besides, if he shared the requisite time with them now, he could go off for a night of partying without having to stop back at home first. If only he could find them.

He kept an eye out for Debbie since she tended to stand out in a crowd.

"Michael!" he heard her yell a moment later.

"I think your mom found us," Brian said.

"What makes you say that?" Michael asked sarcastically.

"Michael!" Debbie yelled again as she pushed her way through the crowd to her son and pulled him in a tight embrace. "My boy is a high school graduate!"

"Hi, Mom."

Debbie finally released her son. "I am so proud of you!"

"Mom, all I did was walk up to the stage and pick up a blank piece of paper."

"That's not what I meant." She gave him a look that only Michael, Brian, and Vic fully understood. "I am so proud of you."

"You did a very mature thing," Vic agreed.

"Hello, Brian," Mrs. Kinney said as she reached her son. She was not forthcoming with hugs in the way that Debbie had been.

"Hi, Mom."

Brian's father didn't even give a "Hello." His mind was elsewhere. "What the hell kind of high school graduation is this? Naked men dancing around on a roof! The principal should be fired for allowing that crap."

Brian did his best not to laugh. He had not only expected this kind of reaction, but had been hoping for it.

Of course, Michael quickly came to the prankster's defense. "It was just a joke, Mr. Kinney."

"Jokes are funny," Mr. Kinney replied. "That was perverse. Whoever pulled that prank is just a pathetic excuse for a kid. He should have his diploma withheld."

"I kind of liked it," Debbie said. "It's been a long time since I saw some young, hot men in their underwear. How about you, honey?" She elbowed Mrs. Kinney in the side.

Brian's mother looked scandalized. He kind of liked the reaction. It was the first real emotion he had seen from her in the longest time.

"And, oh, the last time I did the time warp," Debbie said with a wink to Vic, "well . . . never mind."

"It was just part of the jokes they pull at every graduation, Dad," Claire said. Brian wondered if she suspected he had been the prankster.

"And what about that poor Todd Weaver?" Debbie said, not even bothering to contain her laughter. "It was so horrible when he fell through the stage like that. I think he wound up with a mouthful of dirt."

"Just horrible," Vic agreed with a smile. Brian figured that Debbie had filled her brother in on Todd's tormenting.

Brian's dad did not look amused in the least. "If I were in charge of this school—"

"We've got to get our diplomas," Brian said.

"Missy is having a party," Michael said to his mom. "So you don't have to wait."

"Fine with me, dear." She gave him another hug.

Brian stepped aside to let Michael have a moment alone with his family. Unfortunately, that left Brian alone with his own.

"So you're going to this party?" Mrs. Kinney asked.

"I was planning on it."

"Well, don't you stay out all night," she said rather loudly. Brian suspected that she said it for the benefit of the people standing around. She never said things like that when there wasn't an audience.

A minute later, Brian and Michael headed across the soccer field to the gym where the actual diplomas were being handed out. The mass of students surrounding them were all talking about the end of the ceremony and the go-go boys. Rumors were already beginning to spread about the perpetrator and the boys themselves. Most people had already settled on Missy Caldwell as having pulled together the stunt.

"If they only knew," Michael said after the third person came up to them asserting several reasons why the prankster was definitely Missy.

"It's more fun with them not knowing," Brian said as they reached the gym.

The place was a mob scene. Tables had been set up around the room with homeroom advisers stationed to give out the diplomas to their classes. The intention was that single-file lines would form at the respective tables. The diplomas would then be handed out in an orderly fashion.

This was far from the case.

As soon as Brian entered the room, he realized that this was the last chance he was going to have to see many of the people he had spent some of the most memorable years of his life with. Not everyone was going to Missy's party, but he wasn't sure who was and who wasn't. While it was true that Michael was the only person at that school that he cared for deeply, he would miss many others. Apparently, everyone else realized the same thing as the single-file lines failed to form. Instead the room was full of people in pairs and groups hugging, crying, and trying to act as if this weren't the end.

Even though Brian looked at the criers with a fair amount of contempt, he had to admit to himself that even he was a little moved by the enormity of the moment.

"Wow," Michael said as it hit him as well.

"This could take a while," Brian said. "Let's split up and meet back by the Nova."

"Okay." Michael set off for his homeroom teacher. Brian saw that Harley Milner had stopped Michael after he had only taken three steps.

It took Brian several minutes to cross the gym and reach the table where his homeroom teacher, Mrs. Cooper, was sitting. Along with his diploma, a surprise was waiting for him.

"Congratulations, Mr. Kinney," said the man sitting beside Mrs. Cooper.

"Mr. Palmer," Brian replied, trying to hide his smile. "I didn't expect to see you here."

"I never miss a graduation. And I was hoping to run into you."

"Really?"

"I was disappointed when you didn't show up for the sports banquet. You never got your trophy."

"I had plans," Brian replied, remembering back to the blow job in the front seat of the Nova.

"I'm sure you did," Mr. Palmer said with a knowing look. "Well, I have it in my office, if you'd like to get it."

"Why, yes, Mr. Palmer, I'd like it a lot," Brian said, looking directly into the man's eyes.

The gym teacher got up from the table and led Brian away.

"Brian!" Mrs. Cooper called after him. "Your diploma."

"Oh, yeah." Brian came back to pick up the document.

"Good luck, Mr. Kinney."

"Have a nice life," he replied as he went off with Mr. Palmer.

As he walked out of the gym, Brian caught Michael's eye. Michael was obviously aware of what was going on, especially since he checked his watch and shot Brian a dirty look.

Brian ignored his friend.

The halls outside the gym were empty since the students were only supposed to use the entrance off the field. This made the walk to the gym teacher's office much easier. Brian's graduation gown flowed out behind him as he moved.

"So, Mr. Palmer," Brian said as they walked beside each other. "How does next year's team look."

"You mean since my star player is going off to college?"

"Think you'll be able to fill the void?"

"It might take some work." Mr. Palmer opened the door to his office. "But I'm sure I can find a suitable replacement."

Brian stepped into the office. He had only been in there a few times during his high school career, but the place instantly made him horny. This was not typical of many rooms at Susquehanna High, even though he had experienced his fair share of sex at various locations in the building.

The door closed behind them and Brian heard a familiar click that he knew to be the lock.

"Well, there it is." Mr. Palmer indicated the large trophy on his desk. "Athlete of the Year."

"Why, Gary, it's bigger than I thought it would be." Brian crossed the room. He took off his graduation cap and set it and his diploma down beside the award.

"You deserve it," Gary replied, trying to keep the conversation serious for a moment. "I've never seen a student work so hard at any sport since I started here."

"I had good motivation." Brian rubbed his hand up and down over the trophy. "And a good motivator."

"Come on, Brian. Be serious for a minute. I'm trying to have a talk with you."

"I don't want to be serious." Brian pulled Gary to him. "I want to have fun."

Brian pushed his lips against Gary's. Every pretense of discussion slipped away as the two mouths melded into one another. Kissing was a relatively new addition to their extracurricular activities. They had only done it once or twice before. Brian and Gary had been together no more than a dozen times since their first coupling in the locker room, but each time the sex had progressed to a new level. Gary had insisted that they take it slow because he didn't want to lead Brian on. Brian had never quite managed to convince the guy that he knew exactly what he was doing.

The kiss was both intense and gentle. Brian liked the way Gary kissed. It was not the same hurried attack that boys his own age seemed to excel at. This was slow and methodical, yet with passion nonetheless. It made him even harder in anticipation for what was to come.

Gary broke their embrace. "I think it's time for your graduation present." He pulled at the zipper by Brian's neck. Gary slowly lowered the zipper down Brian's body, making sure to press gently against his clothing as the hand slid down his chest, past his stomach, and over his erect cock straining for release.

The gown was open, revealing Brian's stylish clothing beneath. Gary pulled at the black leather belt and slid it out through the loops. His hands undid the button and pulled at the zipper on Brian's pants. Again, Gary's hand slowly pulled at the metal as he caressed the hardness behind it. Once the zipper's progression halted, Gary took hold of the trousers and pulled them down to Brian's ankles.

Brian leaned back against the desk wearing his shirt, tie, open graduation gown, and red silk boxers. Gary was on his knees, leaning into Brian's crotch. He opened his mouth and clamped gently down on Brian's cock, still within the material of the boxers.

The feeling of mouth and silk stroking his cock was a decadent pleasure. Of course, that feeling was nothing compared to what was about to come next. Brian felt Gary's hand reach into the opening at the front of his boxers. The cool recycled air of the office hit his cock as it was freed from the silken confines of the shorts. But Brian was soon enveloped in warmth again as his cock slid into Gary's mouth.

Brian let out a soft moan as Gary's tongue worked its way down the shaft, tickling the underside. Gary's lips pressed down, squeezing Brian's manhood as saliva moistened the cock. Brian had learned a lot about giving head from his few sessions with Gary. It was the most fun he had ever had in school.

The edge of the desk pressed into Brian's tight ass. Gary's hands were slowly working their way around to fondle the two firm globes. He took each side into his grip as he pulled Brian toward him, allowing for more of the thick cock to slide down his throat.

It was all Brian could do not to let out a loud moan of pleasure as Gary slid the cock out of his mouth and took it in once again. He repeated the motion several times, bringing Brian closer and closer to climax.

"That feels so good," Brian whispered.

Gary moaned in agreement. His hands started working their way toward Brian's ass.

"Oh, yeah," Brian moaned as an index finger hit its mark. He hadn't experienced foreplay this good in a while.

"I'm getting close," he whispered urgently.

He wasn't ready for this to end.

Apparently, neither was Gary as he released the cock from his mouth and stood up. Looking Brian in the eyes once again, Gary slid the graduation gown off Brian's shoulders onto the floor. Brian stepped out of the rest of his clothes. The cool linoleum floor felt good against his bare feet.

The chill did nothing to abate his raging hard-on.

Gary loosened the tie around Brian's neck before slowly sliding it out from his collar. He then took the silk tie and wrapped it loosely around Brian's cock, sliding the silk gently over the bare flesh. It felt even better than the boxers had. Brian decided right there that he was going to be adding a lot of silk to his wardrobe.

The shirt came off last and Brian was entirely nude, leaning up against Gary's desk.

"You look so hot," Gary said as he pulled Brian into another kiss.

Brian's naked body rubbed up against the fabric of Gary's suit. He knew that his leaking cock was leaving a trail of fluid against the cotton pants but figured if Gary didn't care, he shouldn't either.

"This just doesn't seem fair," Brian said as he ended the kiss and slid Gary's jacket off. "Let me return the favor."

Brian slowly removed Gary's clothing one piece at a time. He continued to marvel at the hard body underneath. He suspected that more years of working out would do the same to his.

Once Gary was entirely naked, Brian covered Gary's erect cock with kisses before finally sliding it in past his lips.

Years ago, it had been the first cock he had ever tasted, and it still ranked among the best. Brian mirrored Gary's actions and then threw in an extra few techniques he had learned from the brunet he had been with last Saturday night. The moans of appreciation he heard from above spurred him on to be even more experimental as his hands tightly gripped Gary's ass.

After a few minutes, Brian came up for air and performed a little mouth to mouth.

"This feels so good," Gary moaned.

"It's about to feel much better." Brian leaned Gary against the desk. He saw his pants lying on the floor and bent provocatively to retrieve them, knowing that Gary was enjoying the view. He returned to face Gary with his wallet in hand. A condom was removed from its confines before the leather holder was dropped back to the floor.

He kissed Gary again.

"Put it on me," Gary instructed.

"I had something a little different in mind." Brian leaned into Gary until his bare back was lying against the top of his desk.

"This is new," Gary said excitedly.

Brian lifted Gary's legs onto his shoulders. He slipped a finger into Gary's ass and massaged his pleasure center, then slid the condom onto his own cock. Once he felt Gary loosen up, Brian spit down on his cock and slowly worked his way inside.

The pressure on Brian's cock was wonderful as he slid himself into an envelope of warmth. Inch after inch slipped inside Gary. Both men were breathing heavily. It took nearly a minute for Brian to carefully work himself inside up to the hilt.

"Fuck me," Gary demanded.

And Brian obliged.

Brian pounded himself into Gary, slamming up against the desk. He hammered the man's ass repeatedly with his cock.

Their moans were growing in volume.

Neither of them cared. Brian no longer attended the school.

He leaned forward and kissed Gary hard against the lips. Their tongues jousted as Brian continued to impale Gary with his hard cock. Sweat was forming on both of their bodies as the heat rose in the room.

Brian could feel himself getting closer as his thrusts became more rapid. By the sounds coming from the mouth linked with his, Brian could tell that Gary was enjoying himself too. Brian braced himself as he could feel his balls tightening. Without a thought to anyone's being out in the halls, he let out a massive yell as he shot his load into the condom up Gary's ass.

With their mouths still pressed against each other, Brian heard an echo of the yell and felt several shots of fluid against his stomach.

He had managed to make Gary cum without even touching his cock.

The two naked bodies fell into exhaustion as sweat and cum bound them together. While Brian lay on top, he could feel his spent cock softening until it slipped out of Gary's warm insides. Brian wished that they could share one last shower together, but knew that was out of the question. After several minutes, he finally tore himself away from Gary's body.

"Here." Gary handed Brian a sports towel. Brian used it to wipe the various fluids from his body.

"Thanks." He handed the towel back to Gary. "You can keep it to remember me by."

"I won't forget you," Gary said, pulling on his underwear. "And I don't think you'll forget me either."

Brian chose not to comment as he put his clothes back on.

He knew that Gary was right.

Once both men were dressed, they stopped to have one last look before they went their separate ways. They knew this was the end. Brian was surprised by how little emotion he had over the parting. He had always said that he and Gary were just in it for the fun, but he often suspected there was something more. He even used to secretly be afraid that he was going to develop feelings for Gary that would make going off to college more difficult.

Brian was happy to realize that now that the time had come, he felt none of that. He knew he would certainly miss the sex with Gary, but that was all. He didn't even feel the need to kiss the man good-bye.

"Good luck in college," Gary said. "And have fun."

"Oh, I will, Mr. Palmer." Brian took his trophy and diploma and left the room.

He headed back to the gym to meet up with Michael. The place was emptier than it had been before, and he figured that most of the students had made their way to their respective family gatherings and Missy's party. He dropped off his cap and gown before moving toward the exit and leaving high school for good.

Brian walked out of the gym and let the cool evening air blow away the scent of sex that clung to his body. A world of possibilities lay before him.

A full scholarship awaited him at the most prestigious school in the area.

He would finally be out of his parents' house and free to live the life that he had only been beginning to experience in high school.

Brian dropped his trophy in the trash can beside the gym exit and went off to find his closest friend.

chapter nineteen

Michael hurried up the front steps to his house. His right hand was in his pants pocket fondling the *Batman* tickets excitedly. Only a few more hours and he and Brian would be watching the midnight show of what promised to be the coolest movie of the year.

He had rarely been more excited about a movie.

"I got my tickets!" he said as he came in the front door.

"And I got pictures!" Debbie yelled from the kitchen.

"Great." All the excitement drained right out of his body. It had been a week since graduation and he had finally managed to put the events out of his mind.

Debbie hurried into the living room and sat her son down on the couch. She handed him a Kodak envelope that was overloaded with photos. "These are from the prom and graduation," she said excitedly. "I've already seen them."

Michael took the photos out of the envelope. The first picture was of him and Brian in their tuxedos. He had forgotten how good his friend looked all dressed up.

This one needed to be framed.

"Two of the best-looking young men in Pittsburgh," Debbie said. "You'll be fighting guys off with a stick next year . . . or more likely, a prick!"

"Mom!" Michael exclaimed with embarrassment.

"Oh, grow up." She gave him a playful swat on the arm.

"You're telling *me* to grow up," he said playfully. "That's a good one."

Michael flipped through the photos his mom had taken at both the preprom and pregraduation parties. There were duplicates of each photo. Presumably his mom had made a set for Mrs. Kinney as well. Michael assumed that those would go into some drawer in the Kinney household, never to be seen again. The family didn't exactly have a lot of photos lining the walls.

When Michael reached the first of the photos his mom had taken at the graduation ceremony, he was shocked at how much detail had been captured. His mom's camera must have had an amazing lens. The word FAG on his cap was clear in every single photo. "You have to throw these out."

"I will do no such thing. It's the first time my son proudly proclaimed who he was to the world. A mother likes to remember these things."

"Why, so you can bring it up and embarrass me in social settings?"

"Michael, you should never be embarrassed by who you are. I thought you figured that out at graduation."

"I just didn't want Todd Weaver to think he got one over on me. Stop trying to make this about my place in the world."

"That is exactly what this is about. You're gay. It's not going to get any easier just because you're out of high school. The teasing gets a lot more harsh when it's coming from adults."

"Great. Something to look forward to. As if I didn't have enough already."

"I just meant—"

"I know what you meant," Michael said in a lighter tone. "Just, please don't give those to Mrs. Kinney."

"Don't worry. I don't think that woman would get the point."

Michael continued flipping through the photos, cringing with each one.

"Where's Uncle Vic?"

"He's out with some friends." Debbie's tone grew more serious. "And actually, there's something I wanted to talk to you about."

"Okay." Michael let out a laugh when he reached a photo of Todd Weaver's head sticking out of the stage floor.

"Please put the pictures down, honey."

Michael did as he was told. He had rarely seen his mother with such a grim look on her face before. "What's wrong?"

"It's . . . well . . . I . . ."

And he'd *never* known her to be at a loss for words.

"You're scaring me. Just tell me what it is."

"You know how we've talked about safe sex, right?"

"We have this discussion like once a month, Mom." Michael figured there had to be something more to it than that.

"I was doing laundry a couple weeks ago."

"What's that got to do with anything?"

"I'm easing into a conversation here," she said a little harshly. "Just give me a minute."

"Sorry."

"I found a phone number in the pocket of a pair of your pants. It had a name on it. Max?"

Michael had forgotten all about the guy from Carnegie Mellon he had met on his first trip to Babylon. "I meant to throw that out."

"I don't want you to feel like you have to keep secrets from me. If you met a guy—"

"He's nobody—"

"I just want to know—"

"He's nobody, really."

"If you're having sex, I mean—"

"Mom!" He did not want to get into this conversation. True, he wasn't actually having sex as Brian defined it, but he had had something vaguely within the realm of sex a while back, and he was *not* comfortable talking about it with his mom.

"I mean," she tried to clarify her point, "I want to know if you're being safe."

"If I was having sex—and I'm not saying that I am, because I'm not—but, if I was having sex, I would be as safe as I could be." At least he thought he was being safe. He wasn't sure what precautions he needed to take when having oral sex, but couldn't quite figure out how to ask his mom that question.

"Good."

"Is that what all this is about? Because we've talked about this before and you don't usually act this way when we do."

"Well, there's more." She looked rather pale.

"Okay," he said cautiously.

"It's just . . . sometimes no matter how safe you are, you can't always be sure that your friends are being safe."

"Is this about Brian? I mean, I know he gets around, but I'm pretty sure he's careful."

"Hey, I wash more of his clothes than his own mother. I know he gets around too—"

"So you're saying you have a problem with Brian?" Michael did not like where this conversation was going.

"No," she said, a little too quickly. "I mean, I can tell he lives a bit of a dangerous lifestyle—"

"He's always safe."

"Nothing is one hundred percent safe. But that's not the point."

"What exactly is the point?" he asked, throwing a little

of his own emotional baggage into the conversation. "Do you want me to stop being friends with Brian because of his lifestyle? Well, don't worry, he starts up at Carnegie next week. That should take care of your concerns."

"What are you talking about?" Debbie asked with concern for her son.

"What are you talking about?"

"Are you afraid of losing Brian?"

"I've never *had* Brian."

"I mean as a friend. When he goes away to school."

Silence.

"Carnegie Mellon *is* very different from Allegheny Community." Debbie zeroed in on Michael's main concern. "He'll be living at school. You'll be living at home."

"The school's not that far from here," he said hopefully.

"True. But it is something to think about."

He didn't want to hear his mom agreeing with his concerns.

"Look, Michael. I can't tell you everything's going to be fine and I hate to sound like a cliché—"

"No, you don't," he said with the first smile since seeing the photo of Todd Weaver.

"Okay, no, I don't. You just have to take it one day at a time. Trust me, Brian would be lost without you."

"Right," he said, not believing it for a second.

"Hey, don't argue with your mother. You're the only family that boy has. Trust me, that . . . woman . . . who goes around calling herself his mother isn't even half as close to Brian as you are. He needs you."

Michael thought for a moment about what his mom was saying.

"Thanks," he said, feeling a lot better. It was nice just to finally get his concerns out in the open and to hear that someone understood the whole story. "But that wasn't what you wanted to talk about."

"When's Brian coming to pick you up for the movie?"

"About an hour. What did you want to talk about?"

"It can wait. You boys go off and have fun tonight."

Brian pulled the top drawer out of his desk and dumped the contents into a trash bag without even bothering to check to see what he was throwing out. He repeated the action with the other two desk drawers. The possibility that he was trashing something important didn't even cross his mind.

Once the desk was done, he moved on to the closet. He pushed aside the clothing that he knew he was going to take with him and found little else to dump from there. Brian wasn't much of a pack rat. He tended to find things, use them, and then discard them. It was one of the larger differences between him and Michael.

His best friend was a collector by nature. Michael filled his room with action heroes and toys while his mom's garage was packed with boxes of old comic books. He kept insisting that the comic books would be worth something someday, but Brian knew that was not the reason for the collection. Michael liked to hold on to the memories of his childhood. Brian wanted nothing more than to move on to adulthood.

Brian did find his stash of gay porn in the back of the closet—the magazines that he used to sneak into the house when he was still a freshman at Susquehanna. Brian didn't need to rely on photos of men for inspiration anymore. He could get the real thing whenever he wanted.

The dirty magazines joined the rest of his childhood in the trash.

"What the hell are you doing?" his father asked as he came in the room without bothering to knock.

For a moment, Brian thought his dad had seen the magazines, but then assumed the reaction would have been more violent if that were the case.

"Cleaning."

"What's the matter, *son*," his dad said, slurring his *s*'s. "Can't wait to get out of here?"

Brian could smell the beer on his dad's breath from across the room. Jack Kinney was a practiced drinker, meaning it took quite a few belts before he reached the slurring stage. Brian glanced at the clock. His father had started drinking much earlier than usual.

"Just wanted to tidy a few things up," Brian said, tying the trash bag. He wanted to get it out into the can before his dad decided to go snooping just for the hell of it. Brian ignored his father as he took the trash downstairs and out to the curb. He had started cleaning because trash was collected the following morning and he was hoping that his stuff would be gone before anyone noticed. When Brian returned to the house, he found his father waiting in the living room.

"I asked you a question, boy."

Brian knew that he should just play along with his dad as the agreeable son and answer the questions as they were asked. But Brian hated his father's condescending tone, especially since it was so undeserved.

"And what question was that?"

"I wanted to know if you couldn't wait to get out of here."

"And I said I was just tidying up."

"Tidying up," his dad repeated in a mocking tone. "Isn't that just quaint. Next thing you know you'll be having tea with the ladies."

"Excuse me," Brian said, going back upstairs.

He could hear his father's footsteps behind him. "Stop walking away from me, boy!"

"Stop being such an ass, Dad!" Brian yelled once he was back in his room.

Jack swung a fist in the direction of his son.

Brian jumped to the side and his father missed him by a good foot.

"You want to try that again?" Brian asked, taking a defensive stance.

Brian knew that his father had a penchant for violence.

But like everything else in the Kinney household, this too was ignored. Brian had no doubt that he could easily defend himself if his father actually tried to threaten him physically. He would never let it come to that, however. That would bring him down to his dad's level.

That was a place he never intended to go.

Brian made a decision right then and there. He grabbed his suitcase from under the bed.

"You think you're so much better than me," Jack said, reading his son's mind. "Getting a scholarship to the university. You think I don't know what you're up to."

"I'm *up to* getting a good education," Brian said as he went into the closet.

"You want to make your dad look like an idiot. Waving around your education and your scholarship."

"You know, it's funny. Most fathers would be proud of their sons when they did well." Brian grabbed an armload of clothes and threw them into the suitcase without worrying about wrinkling anything. He went back and grabbed some shoes, making sure that he took the Ferragamos.

"Most sons wouldn't shove it in their father's faces." His father slurred the last few words.

Brian truly had no idea what had brought this on. He hadn't shoved anything in anyone's face. That was the main problem living with his father. These little vignettes came out of nowhere.

But Brian didn't have to put up with his father's crap anymore.

He slammed the suitcase shut.

"Where the hell are you going?"

Brian saw Michael's yearbook sitting on his dresser. He picked it up and threw it under his arm. *"Carnegie Mellon University,"* he said, stressing each word. "The place that proves I'm better than you."

"Why you little shit." His father lunged for him.

Again, his father missed. This time, he lost his balance and fell onto the bed. There was nothing worse than a sloppy drunk.

Brian looked at his dad for a moment.

He had nothing more to say.

Brian grabbed his suitcase with his free hand and walked out into the hall. When he passed his parents' room, he saw his mom sitting silently on the edge of her bed. He leaned in the doorway, waiting for her to say something.

"The dorms don't open until Monday" was all she at last said.

"I'm sure I can find someone willing to put me up until then." He stormed down the stairs and out of the house.

Brian went out to the street, unlocked the Nova's trunk, and threw his suitcase inside along with Michael's yearbook.

It had all happened so quickly, Brian wasn't even sure how it had started.

He looked back at the house. He still had a good chunk of his wardrobe left inside, but he had no intention of going back to get it. Those things would just have to wait for a time when his dad wasn't going to be around. Brian knew that he hadn't ended his relationship with his father, but he had certainly put up a larger wall between them. And most of what had happened would be forgotten when the alcohol wore off. He pushed that thought out of his mind as he considered where he was going to spend the night.

The answer seemed obvious when he looked at the bracelet on his wrist. But Brian had something to prove. He had no doubt that he could find some guy—or guys—willing to put him up over the next few days until the dorm opened. It might even be a fun challenge to stay in a different place each night. So much for his rule never to go home with strangers. But the real excitement behind the idea was that it was the last thing his father would ever want—not that the man would ever know.

Brian slammed the trunk shut. He looked back at the house one last time and saw his sister watching him from the window.

"Brian!" a voice called from down the street.

Brian turned away from Claire and saw Michael hurrying toward him. He almost smiled when he noticed that Michael was carrying Brian's yearbook, but that would have lifted his foul mood, so he kept the scowl he was working on. This unexpected turn of events made things more difficult. Brian had wanted to make a clean break and start his new life, but his old life was running down the street.

"Glad I caught you," Michael said as he reached the Nova. "I was so excited that I couldn't wait."

"For what?"

"*Batman!* I'm sure the line is already forming for the midnight show. I thought we should get there early."

Brian had forgotten about the movie.

"About that—" Brian started to say.

"I've heard that Jack Nicholson is amazing as the Joker," Michael rambled on with excitement. "This is going to be so cool. Michael Keaton's supposed to be a pretty good Batman too, but I don't know. I mean, *Beetle Juice* is one thing but—"

"I don't know if I'm really in the mood for Batman and Robin tonight."

Michael looked crushed. "Robin's not in the movie."

"Oh, right, isn't he like dead in the comic books?" Brian searched his memory for some vague piece of information Michael had once mentioned. "So much for Dick Grayson."

"No, that was Jason Todd, the second Robin. Dick Grayson is still alive but now goes by the name . . . You don't really care about any of this, do you?"

Brian gave the question serious thought for a moment. He honestly didn't care about the status of comic book characters, but he couldn't help but understand the importance of the subject matter to Michael. As much as Brian couldn't wait for the next stage of his life to begin, he knew that Michael was holding on to the current stage with a tight grip.

Brian began to think that maybe that wasn't the worst thing in the world. It would be nice to live in a world with comic book heroes and villains for a while longer. And the Novotny home was as safe a haven as any Batcave could be.

"I already got the tickets," Michael said with less enthusiasm.

"Well, if you already paid, I wouldn't want them to go to waste."

Michael's face immediately lit up. "You're going to love it. It's totally dark and brooding."

"Kind of like me."

"You're nothing like that at all. Anyway, I brought your yearbook back. I signed it."

Brian took the book from Michael. He realized that something was working in his favor. "I have yours right here." He reopened the trunk and pulled it out.

The look of excitement on Michael's face was priceless.

Brian could feel himself giving in to the contagious mood. "Get in. If we go now, we can be first in line."

"That's why I'm here." Michael hopped in the car.

Brian got in the driver's side and started the car.

Some crappy tune blasted out of the radio.

"I almost forgot," Michael yelled over the music. He leaned forward and worked the knobs. "I found this new AM station."

Static filled the car for a minute as Michael zeroed in the dial. After what seemed like an eternity, actual music filled the air. It was Modern English, a group probably never heard on Pittsburgh AM radio ever before.

Brian looked at his friend and smiled. He pulled his car out onto the road and headed for the movies.

There's nothing you and I won't do
I'll stop the world and melt with you

Dear Brian,

You have helped me through so much these past four years. If it weren't for you, I wouldn't be who I am today. I mean that in a good way. I can't begin to thank you for the many ways you've affected my life so I won't even try. Just know that whatever happens in the future, you will always be a part of me. I hope that you and I remain friends for the rest of our lives . . . If only we had more time in which to be young.

Love,
Michael

Dear Michael,

Remember, with you, it's real. With everyone else, it's just all about sex.

Love,
Brian

Don't miss SEASON 3 of
queer as folk

Order SHOWTIME today and
get $25 cash!

Plus, the very best entertainment...anywhere!

Hollywood Hits No One Else Has®

Bold Original Pictures and Series

To subscribe:
call 1-800-SHOWTIME
or log on to SHO.com